DANCE OF THE MOURNING CLOAK

CJ WARRANT

Enjoy!

Dance of the Mourning Cloak

Part of the Dark Hollow Lake Collection

By Cruel Ink Publication

Copyright © 2021 by CJ Warrant

Cover Art by Anne Berkeley

✷ Created with Vellum

While Waiting for Thee:

Don't weep at my grave, for I am not there,
I've a date with a butterfly to dance in the air.
I'll be singing in the sunshine, wild and free,
Playing tag with the wind, while I'm waiting for thee.
~ We are as the wings of a butterfly,
bound together with the love of God~
Jenn, The Butterfly Box

CONTENTS

PROLOGUE

EARLY OCTOBER IN ALTOONA
PENNSYLVANIA

Chase Bishop

It was clearing midnight when I pulled up to the back of the building I called home for the past three years. Exhaustion rang out of me from a lack of sleep in the last twenty-four hours. Still, I clung to the handrail like a lifeline and ascended the back staircase to the shitty apartment I shared with my sister Cassie above Donovan's Secondhand Shop in Altoona.

I knew it wasn't much, but it was enough for what my salary could afford. I had a good landlord, and it was a decent enough place for my kid sister.

Three days on the road was too much for me. The weariness nearly bit through my sanity like a hungry dog with a mangled chew toy. I gathered what I could from my zapped energy and fought each step until I reached the front door.

The next time Drake tossed me that run again, I had to decline the load. The amount of stress wasn't worth the payout for Cassie and me. With her autism spectrum disorder, the only person she felt comfortable being around was me. The double-edged sword of my obligation where Cassie was concerned was at my jugular. If I moved in either direction, my throat would be the one cut.

Don't get me wrong. I loved my sister so much that I would do anything for her. Though for all it was worth keeping her safe and me sane, I was burnt out mentally and physically from those responsibilities thrust onto my shoulders from age eighteen. Younger, if you looked at how we grew up in an abusive household.

As my feet hit the final step, I took out my key to unlock the front door. The second my eyes landed on the slightly jarred door, my heart stuttered to a near halt. Without thought, I pulled out my bug-out knife tucked inside my jean jacket pocket and flipped it open. With a booted foot, I slowly pushed the weathered door all the way open and carefully walked inside the six hundred square foot apartment.

The cushions on the dingy grey couch that separated the living room and the kitchen were ripped to shreds. Someone tore out the innards and looked inside the cavity for something. I don't know what.

If the burglars were looking for money, they were in the wrong place. The only things anyone would find here was old dust bunnies and possibly some dead cockroaches. No cash.

It seriously pissed me off as I looked about my place. I worked damn hard keeping us above the poverty line. But now, my stuff was strewn around the room as though a tornado had torn through the apartment.

Careful not to touch anything, I stepped over shattered dance figurines that meant something to Cassie. She was going to be righteously upset since those statuettes were our mother's. My sister cherished them like they were family. Now, they were trash.

Several broken picture frames littered the floor too. Underneath the broken glass harbored carefree smiles. Happy faces of Cassie and my mother, Barbara Bishop, died of unknown causes when I was fourteen. Unknown, because our father never told us how our mother died. There was never a funeral or a wake to say goodbye either—only a memorial, which lasted about an hour. Cassie and I never had a chance to mourn our mother. Because if we did, we got it bad from our father.

Before I took another step, my attention automatically fixed on the kitchen's worn yellow linoleum. My gut twisted tight like two wrestling pythons fighting over a prey as I stared down at Cassie's bedazzled butterfly purse lay haphazardly on the floor.

The alarm bells rang in my head, warning me something wasn't right. That purse should have been with Cassie at John's house. Not here.

God damn it, Cassie. Don't be here. Please don't be here.

I would rather deal with a break-in than have something happened to my sister.

I snatched my cell phone from the front pocket of my filthy jeans and dialed the only number I knew by heart. Two rings, John Vaughn, my old man's ex-partner from the police force, answered in a hasty breath. "Chase."

"Is Cassie with you?" I clipped out in a rush while my eyes gathered the rest of the damage around me.

"No. She took off on me a couple of hours ago. I went to your place, but the apartment was empty," John said, with resolve in his voice that didn't ease the worry worming further into my brain.

"Damn it, John. You promised to keep an eye on her.

How did she slip past you?" My anger was turning into a rolling boil.

"You know your sister. She might have ASD, but she's a smart cookie." The hollow chuckle from John only pissed me off more.

"What the hell? Cassie taking off isn't some joke. I'm at the apartment now, and it looks like someone broke in," I hissed. "Tell me she left her purse here when you came and got her." The silence over the line made my heart ratcheted up to the point my chest hurt from the thrashing organ. "John," I said almost a plea and held my breath for his reply.

"Sorry, son. Cassie took her purse with her."

"Fuck!" I hadn't meant to scream into the phone, but the intense fear for my twenty-five-year-old sister was splintering my sanity.

I regretted asking John to watch over Cassie while I worked, but he was the only one I remotely trusted with my sister. Now, Cassie took off on him without a hint of where she could be.

Though, I had hope. When Cassie was younger, she would take off and headed straight to a park a few blocks from our home. Staring down at her purse, the dread that infiltrated my reasonings was telling me that wasn't the case this time.

I would rather have Cassie wandering the streets instead of facing down a burglar who could hurt her, or worse.

With swelling panic, I called out her name. "Cassie." Those two syllables knocked the breath out of my lungs with increasing silence. "Cassie, I'm home. Come out." I demanded this time.

My eyes automatically landed on the bi-fold closet doors. When Cassie had her episodes—when the world got to be too much for her, which seemed to be more prevalent these days, she hid in the closet where she felt safe. It was her shelter.

I yanked open the cheap louver doors and attempted to coax her out. "Cassie, it's Chase. Come on out, Sissy." I used her nickname, hoping she would pop her head out and show herself.

Nothing. The closet was untouched.

With the growing silence, the golf ball size lump in my throat just got bigger. I quickly checked the bathroom, then my bedroom. Still nothing. With each empty step, my panic began to engulf me. I stared down the short hallway to Cassie's room . I strode to the shut door and paused. Cassie hated her door closed. It stemmed from all the years my father locked her in her room.

The last thing Cassie needed was to see was me panicked. So I sucked in a breath to ease my rapid heartbeat, but it didn't help.

I turned the dull glass knob and uttered her name. "Cassie?" My whisper went unanswered. If Cassie was in one of her episodes, the last thing she did was talk.

As my eyes tried to adjust to the darkness of the tiny space, the vibrantly painted butterflies vibrated off the walls. Cassie's favorite wind chimes that hung in the corner cast odd-shaped shadows about the small room, with the help of a partially open window and the glow of the moon filtering into the room.

"What the…" my words faltered as my eyes were playing tricks on me. "Butterflies?" Not the shadows from the chimes, but actual live butterflies flitted about in the dark. I thought I saw a hint of color that faded into black. That wasn't possible.

With Cassie's name on my lips, I flipped on the light and saw nothing. No butterflies. Just the homemade wind chimes she made a few years ago. I had to be going crazy. Then my attention slowly gravitated to the floor, and every muscle in my body froze. There, Cassie's crumpled body was at the foot of the bed like a broken doll.

"Cassie." Her name tore from my lips in a shout. I dropped to her side, wasn't sure where to touch her. "Damn it, Sissy."

Her beautiful long wheat-colored hair was drenched in blood. It lay sodden on the floor. Red was the only color I saw around my baby sister. Purple and black bruises covered her face, and there was blood down her jawline. But what made my stomach lost its contents were the stab wounds to her chest. They were vicious. Brutal.

I touched her neck, praying for a pulse, but all I felt was the clammy coldness of her pale skin. No life coursed through her veins.

"Oh, Cass, why didn't you stay with John?" The demand came with a torrent of tears that blurred my vision. My sister's cornflower blue eyes stared blankly up at the off-white crackled ceiling. Cassie's mouth gaped open like she had tried to scream for help, but it was too late.

I was too fucking late to save her. I scooped Cassie into my arms, not giving a Goddamn about the blood and cradled her head in the crook of my neck like I used to when she was little or when she was coming down from an episode. Her cold cheek branded my heated sweaty skin as I rocked her slowly in my arms.

"Cassie..." I choked out her name, my mind not believing she was dead. "Talk to me, baby girl. I'm home. Show me your beautiful colors." My mouth felt cotton-filled. Dry and suffocating. I couldn't breathe in an ounce of calm.

My tears bled from my eyes and melded with the blood in her hair. "Wake up," I uttered to Cassie.

I attempted to stand but slipped on the bloody floor. My legs buckled and crashed down onto my knees. Pain shot through my joints, but I didn't a fuck. Someone took my sister from me, and it was my fault she died.

I cradled Cassie's limp form tighter to me, where I knew she would have found it safe. As I continue to rock her back and forth, something dropped out of her left hand. It looked like a square card. Before I got a chance to see what it was, I heard pounding footsteps behind me.

"Jesus H. Christ," John hissed as he stormed into the room. "You have to put her down, Chase. I have too—"

"She's gone, John. Cassie's dead." I cut him off in a cry that drew from my soul. "Who could have done this? She was harmless," I broke out as I got to my feet, but I slipped again, and my back slammed against the wall. "Who fucking killed her, John? Why? Why didn't you watch her closely? You promised me you'd keep her safe." Anger and pain rose sharp that I wouldn't hold back. Couldn't be contained. I aimed all those sharp taloned words of blame at the older man.

"Look at me, Chase. Put Cassie down. I need to see her," John growled out, grabbing my arms and pulling me forward. My eyes locked in a battle with John's. They were angry and lost, mirroring mine. I couldn't look at him anymore. With a blurry gaze at my sister, I finally lowered her back down on the wooden floor.

"You know your sister, Chase. This wasn't the first time she took off on me. But..." John placed shaky fingers to her neck. "Damn it. It's not your fault, or mine."

I couldn't believe what I was hearing. John blamed Cassie. "Are you seriously telling me that this was all her fault?" I gritted out. My rage refused to let another tear fall. As I wiped the remnants of wetness on my cheeks away with the back of my hand, I demanded, "We have to call the police."

"I am the police," John insisted, his eyes narrowed on me.

"No. You're too close to this," I countered, knowing damn well how the protocol worked. Even though my old man was a mean old fuck, I listened and learned because my father had broken most of the rules.

John shook his head and uttered low, "No, Chase. We can't. I will take care of this. I promise."

I wasn't sure if I heard him correctly. "Cassie was murdered. I want the bastard that did this to her to pay."

John stood, eyes hard, and I was the target. "If you call the police, they will implicate you in her murder, and I can't have that. I promised your mother I'd protect you and your sister."

"That doesn't make any sense, John." I wrangled back to my feet, needing to be eye level with the man. "You're not making any fucking sense. We need to call the cops," I repeated.

"I'll do it," John finally snapped. "I'll take care of this. Take what you need and get out of here." He shoved a thick folded-up wad of bills in my right hand. "Get out of Altoona. Buy a burner phone and call me in three days. Once I have all this handled, I'll call you back home. But give me time to clear this up for you and Cassie."

I stared at John as though the man had lost his damn

mind because he had. John's plan was fucked up. No part of what he asked me to do was right. "If I leave, it's a sure thing I'll look guilty." I grated out.

"I said I'll handle it! Don't you trust me?" John snarled. His deep brown eyes were stormy and volatile.

"No," I bit out.

"You're just like your old man, stubborn and obstinate. Chase," he said my name in earnest, that stony edge was gone from his voice. "I promise, you'll be in the clear. Trust me."

"I-I don't know." Yet, the determination on John's face settled something inside me to relent. "Fine—okay." Those words tasted foul on my tongue, but I did trust John for all that was worth.

"Then leave, Chase." His sharp words were back, like a crack to the face. I was momentarily stunned as I stared down at Cassie's broken body and spotted the ill-forgotten card. I stared at the blood-smeared corner. On it was a handwritten date, time, and a place called Sevier Mines. Something was niggling the back of my head to pick it up because it was necessary.

I knew I had only seconds, but I dropped next to Cassie. On my knees , I snagged the card and palmed it. The moment my skin touched the paper, a slight sizzle zapped into my hand and up my arm. For a stunning moment, a brief flash of real butterflies—similar to my sister's wind chimes flitted about in the corner of the room. Was I delusional? I can't be seeing real butterflies. I shoved the momentary lack of focus back and shook my head. Although, I buried the image down deep into the dark recesses of my mind, I could never forget it.

My eyes landed on Cassie. I didn't know how to say goodbye to my sister—not this way. Before I uttered a word or show John the card, he grabbed my arm and hoisted me to my feet. "Go," he thundered. "Get safe." That command and push toward the hallway were enough to get my feet moving.

Still, nothing made sense to me. Not my sister's death, or the way John was acting, and certainly not following my gut to stay. Instead, I ignored it all, grabbed a backpack, crammed what I could inside it, and took off. There was only one place I was heading. The front of the card read, Dark Hollow Lake Reality, in Dark Hollow Lake, Tennessee. In this town, was where I would find the answers. No matter what, I wanted justice for my sister.

CHASE

EIGHT DAYS LATER

"Damn it." A hiss left my lips as I dropped the searing radiator cap like a hot frying pan. If it wasn't for the dirty rag 1 found it in the glove compartment, my hand would have burned into one giant-size blister.

The steam from the busted radiator ribboned into the cool autumn air like a ghostly vapor. Eerie and white. It matched my own exhaled breath leaving my lungs.

The wind kicked up in an aggressive rush around me, hurling yellow, orange, and red leaves in the air. The weather seemed unreasonably cold for October in Tennessee, but how should 1 know since this was my first time in the state. I wished I packed the heavier jacket instead of the zippered hoodie tied around my body. The chill reached down to my bones, making me shiver where I stood.

I was tired of running and wished I could head back home and bury my sister properly.

What made me on edge was not knowing what was going on back home. The last response from John was stomping on my last nerve. He did tell me to call him in three days, but I couldn't wait. And the second I got a burner phone, I called. All I got was his voice mail, and nothing since.

Exhaustion was finally catching up to me. Eight long days on the run without a pause was finally catching up to me.

But now this.

I glared down at the engine of the old crappy blue pickup truck I stole from a farmer outside of Greensboro. I raked a hand through my short, cropped hair in frustration. Frustration and anger flooded my veins as I looked down at the gurgling and hissing machinery as it tried to stay running. The knocking ceased, and a final plume of steam from the radiator released into the night air, like it took its last breath.

I shook my head at my circumstances. It wasn't enough I lost my sister, but fate threw me under the bus. Here I stood, stranded in the middle of backwoods near a town I didn't know anything about to find the woman who *might* have answers to Cassie's murder.

I couldn't call on anyone for help. One, I didn't anyone, aside from John. And two? My cell had died an hour back. The rate I was going, someone would find me dead in these woods unless the animals got a hold of my sorry hide.

What a way to be under the police radar?

Why hadn't I stopped twenty miles back when I knew the truck was in trouble? Instead, I ignored the sputter of the engine until it became an explosive hot water fissure.

The harvest moon overhead lit up the dense woods outlining the adjacent road, which made the scene more of a horror movie than real life. The moon was bright enough to walk the rest of the way to Dark Hollow Lake. But how long would it take me and would I make it there?

I stuck a hand in the pocket of my jeans and felt for the crumpled edge of stiff paper. I pulled it out and stared down at it. I didn't know what possessed me not to tell John about the card. I had ample time to show him. But, something inside told me to keep that bit of information to myself.

My fingertip grazed along with the bubbled lettering of the real estate agent's name, trying to think if that name rang any bells in my head, now that I was able to think more clearly. However, the longer I thought, the more of a tension headache I was getting.

I turned it over and studied the handwriting on the backside of the card once more. The date and time were for five days from now. And under no exceptions, I needed to be at Sevier Mines to uncover the truth about my sister's death.

I blew out a breath, slid the card back into my wallet, and went back glaring at the rusty engine. I dropped the hood and unraveled my hoodie from around my waist, and put it on. Once zipped, I grabbed the backpack from the passenger side. I slung the bag over my shoulder and started walking in the direction of Dark Hollow Lake.

As I set an even pace, every so often, I glanced back to the dilapidated truck and watched the darkness swallow up the vehicle.

The road bent slightly to the left, where the woods thickened. The moonlight couldn't penetrate through the heavy copse of trees on the edge of the road.

As the sounds of crickets chirped to the owls rare hoots, the black pavement under my boot feet took me deeper into the woods.

Everything seemed to be in harmony, except for me. I was the only odd animal that didn't belong on this road —in these woods—at this time of the night. It was as though the blackness was trying to eat me up and devour me whole. Would it be justice for not keeping my sister safe?

Shaking off those dower thoughts, the sounds around me suddenly ceased for five long beats as my breath were seized in my lungs. Trepidation began to trickle in as my imagination was playing tricks on me, like the real butterflies I saw in Cassie's room.

I felt like prey. Something in the shadows along the tree line was hunting me.

I fought each step as my ears stayed tuned to the weird silence. I ignored my growing consternation and kept my rigid pace until I heard the sounds seeping back in.

I breathed in and out and let the burn from my lungs ease. I was never fearful of the night, only what held inside it. Cassie had hated being in the dark. She never felt safe, no matter the circumstances. Our father's drunken rages did that to her. That man had terrorized both of us, especially Cassie, to the point that she never slept through the night, not without a night light.

I, on the other hand, when Henry Bishop had turned himself into ash from a cigarette he had been smoking and ultimately burned himself up, peace never felt better. That bastard deserved what he got for all the torment he brought to his kids and to his dead wife.

Focus, damn it!

Thinking of a man who's been dead for over nine years was ridiculous. With one step at a time, I concentrated on the road of ahead.

As I followed the road to the right, a rush of dried

leaves in a small open clearing caught my attention. The fiery reds, yellows, and oranges swirled around in a cyclone pattern along with the mist-soaked ground. I paused to watch, but only for a second when the hairs on the back of my neck rose sharp, like cold fingers grazing my hairline. I quickly looked around me as the feeling of being watched snapped me back to alert.

As another whirl of icy wind brushed past me, my skin tightened into gooseflesh—a familiar hint of sweet lilac, and something underlying skimmed the air. To me, it smelled like a funeral parlor. The flowers reminded me of death, which was suffocating.

"Hello," I called out, but only the faint echo of my voice reverberated back. "This is fucking nuts." Shaking off the urge to run, I strode forward with purpose in my gate. With another ten or twenty steps under me, the symphony of bugs stopped playing altogether, and all I heard was the pounding of my heart and the rush of blood pooling in my ears. Something wasn't right here, and I didn't care to know either.

There were bigger things to worry about than what was in the woods. I had to get to town and settle in for the night somewhere.

I took another step and stopped dead in my tracks. In the open field to the right of me, a plume of whitish fog crept over the earth like a ghostly apparition and headed toward me. The thick mist illuminated the dying yellowish ferns that dotted the ground. Dead logs of elm and maple trees were scattered about resembling a long ago logger's field. Leaves of various shades of decay shifted abnormally in a slow swirling dance.

Not able to take my eyes off of the scene, I shuddered as a chill snaked up my spine while the mist whirled around and covered my feet. My hands were suddenly frozen like they were dipped in ice water, and my feet were cemented in place.

Overwhelming dread suddenly came over me. My mind warned me to keep walking, head straight, and eyes on the road ahead. But my feet wouldn't move. Like an invisible rope tied around me, it kept pulling me toward that mist. Not able to ignore it any longer, I moved to the edge of the hard pavement and yellowed grass. I skimmed the open field to find... something.

What am I searching for?

To my surprise, in the middle of the small expanse stood a boy. Like magic, he came out of the mist. But that was impossible.

He was dressed in black basketball shorts and a maroon ironman t-shirt. He had to be no more than ten or twelve years old. If my brain could grapple up some sense, I would see this as another illusion my imagination conjured up. Sorry to say, I haven't been thinking clearly since Cassie's death.

The boy's sorrowful dark eyes bore into me like a honed blade. Yet, what drew my panic upon its hackles was there was no barrage of colors around him I usually saw around a person. A faded grey slated hue surrounded him, with only a hint of black around the edges. That wasn't possible. Everyone had colors, no matter how terrible of a person.

Wait. Were those butterflies over his head? I rubbed my eyes and looked again, but they were gone. That was twice I imagined those things.

My attention was back on the boy. The sadness across his face was so apparent that it was palpable in the dense air around us. I almost forgot about his lack of colors around him and the butterflies because I focused on the tears coating his ashen cheeks. I took a step closer as the boy reached out a hand, begging me to come closer like he needed my help.

Like a moth to the flickering flame, I couldn't tear my eyes away. With everything in me, I staunched the overwhelming need to run to him. Those few tentative steps I took were small, but I found myself several feet from the road, away from the safety of the asphalt.

I was terrified, but for some reason, I wasn't afraid enough to walk to him. Even though, something in the back of my mind warned me to run the other way I kept moving toward the boy.

With both arms extended out, the boy called out my name. "Chase." That alone seriously scared the shit out of me.

"How do you know my name?" I said with a shudder.

He opened his mouth, but no words came out. As I took another step, the sounds of a honking horn snared my attention while two giant orbs of light blinded me. I threw my hands up to cover my face as though it would protect me from the impact. One second, I stood in the strange field, and next, pain shot through my body as I hit the ground, and everything faded to black.

2

MELINDA

"Are you crazy standing in the middle of the road? I almost ran you over," I shouted in total panic at the guy came out of nowhere and was now sprawled out on the dirt patch next to my car.

God, did I kill him?

My heart choked to a near stop. My chest hurt to breathe in as I rounded the corner of my Kia Sportage and spot the man before me. He wasn't moving.

"Shit. Shit—Shit! Please be alive. Please, please-please be alive." I leaned down, air caged tight in my lungs, my fingers went to his pulse point. "Oh, thank God." He had a strong pulse.

I took a second, gathered my strength and courage, bent down and carefully rolled the man over onto his back. His face turned away from the headlights, casting a grim shadow over the partially hidden features.

"Please be okay." I lightly shook him, "Hey, are you alright?" but he didn't move. I attempted again. "Sir. Wake up."

A sudden chill went through me, and my spine

snapped straight. I looked around, feeling an odd sense of being watched. I wouldn't say I liked these parts of the woods because I didn't like anything spooky.

"Please wake up, guy." I shook the man harder this time but he wasn't responding.

"Dang it, Melinda. Think. What should I do?"

Jeez, now I'm talking to myself like I'm some crazy nut job.

I looked down at the man I nearly ran over with my car and wondered if he was a nut job too since he was here, in the middle of the woods. And alone.

If I should leave him here and drove to the sheriff's office for help… That wasn't going to do. I couldn't call anyone since my idiot self left the charger on the counter at home, and my phone was dead.

A groan came from the man, which startled me. I shuffled back a few steps, just in case he was some murdering nut bag and I had time to escape in my car.

The nut bag groaned again and slowly turned his head to the point I could see his entire face. To my surprise, he was handsome. But so was Ted Bundy.

"Fuck," he slurred out the swear. "What happened?"

"I sort have hit you with my car—What were you doing in the middle of the road?—Are you lost?" I needed to quit talking, but I couldn't help myself when I'm nervous. "Are you some crazed mental patient?"

"Crazed mental patient?" he repeated. "No. But the boy." A look of bewilderment slid on his face as he rubbed his head.

"What? What boy?" I looked around, making sure I didn't hit his companion too.

Oh God.

I spun around but saw nothing. A small amount of relief coursed through me. But If I didn't hit the boy, where was he? I hoped the boy wasn't going to creep up on me, and kill me where I stood.

I looked down and, "Crap." The man was out again. Maybe I should leave him.

Then I heard my mother's voice rattling in my head. *'Can't leave him there, Melinda. Help him like the good person you are.'*

Am I a good person? "Dang it." I rolled my eyes up to the heavens and knew I was going to regret this.

Without pondering on about my stupid decision, I pulled my car closer to the unconscious man. I opened the passenger side door and carefully dragged him across the edge of the grass, over the small section of gravel, and finally across the strip of the road before I hauled his heavy form into my car. "At least I'm getting my workout in. Jeez, this guy is weighing a ton."

After a good five or so minutes getting him into the car, I finally got him situated in the seat before snapping the seatbelt over his slumped body. I blew out an exhausted but relieved breath.

"You need to lose some weight, buddy—Darn it—I think I have a hernia now," I groaned, rubbing my lower back. I closed the passenger door making sure not to slam it against his head slanted toward the door. I wiped my hands down my jeans and tried shaking off the nervous anxiety anchored in my chest. Taking a glance over the area, I made sure I wasn't missing anything of his.

Putting the car in the drive, I prayed that this stranger wasn't some crazed killer I just saved and that I wouldn't be in trouble with the law.

3

CHASE

Spears of light gouged my eyeballs like pickaxes. I opened my lids with caution and froze in place as pain lanced through my head as spikes of daylight blinded me, which was giving me a headache. With fingers to my right temple, I pressed until the pain eased.

Once the ache dissipated, I opened my eyes and looked around the unfamiliar space. I slowly sat up, but my vision swam, and stalled from moving. With all the muted grey in the room, I held my head as though it would stop the walls from spinning in circles. I leaned back against the headboard and took in several deep breaths until I finally regained some of my stability.

Not sure what happened to me, but I was quite sure I wasn't dead. Then clarity came to me like crystal as the memory of what happened cleared—a car. A woman was babbling nonsense. Nothing was making any sense in my head, except for those headlights were coming at me. Someone... The driver almost killed me. As I moved, pain lanced at my left side. "Shit. Was I was hit by a car?"

I carefully and gently swung my legs down to the floor. I straightened and sat up enough to glance over to the nightstand. The digital clock read ten o'clock, which I was guessing had to be a.m. because of all the light from the window. Still, I wasn't sure where I was, but no matter. It was time for me to get the hell out of here.

I climbed out of bed to search for my clothes. I went through the small dresser that stood next to an empty closet. Not a stitch of my clothing was found—not even my shoes—or my bag. I stared down at the loose pair of grey shorts and baggy white t-shirt I had on and decided it would have to do until I found my clothes.

"Where am I?" I uttered under my breath while I slowly bent and looked under the bed, hoping to see my stuff.

"Mr. Bishop, you're finally up." A woman's voice boomed from the other side of the room, jolting me upright. I cautiously rose from my kneeled position and stared at the beautiful woman with dark brown hair and the purest blue eyes. A swirl of dull blue and yellow with a slight tinge of grey tugged the edges of her aura. She was afraid of me. But not enough that she cautiously skirted the bed and stood several feet from me.

"Who are you?" I asked evenly, trying not to add more to her fear.

"My name is Melinda and you're in my home," she said with small smile, but a note a trepidation was there.

"And where is your home? What town?" I pushed since my memory had some missing gaps. "How did I get here?"

"You're in Dark Hollow Lake," she said. My mouth dropped open in surprise. "Close your mouth, or you'll attract flies," she said with a hint of strain in her voice. Then her words hit me.

"I'll what?" I wasn't sure if I heard her correctly. "Flies?"

"Attract flies. Well, that's what my mamma used to tell me." Her southern lilt became stronger.

Not taking my eyes off of her. "How do you know my name?" I asked with hesitation.

"You told me your name last night. Don't you remember? Now, I'm sorry, but I sort-a peeked into your wallet too and saw for your drivers license to confirm. You can't be too careful nowadays." The corner of her mouth tipped down. "Anyway, I'm babbling. Like I said I'm Melinda, and you are Chase Bishop. Now we got that out of the way; let's get to the real questions. Do you remember what happened last night? And why were you in the middle of the road? You could have been killed."

I let out a huff of breath at her bombarding questions. I ran a hand across my sore scalp and vaguely remembered what happened. "Only bits and pieces. You tell me what happened." A light thrum of pain started radiated at my temples again. I rubbed it gently to ease the ache, but that didn't help this time. Then I remembered the twin orbs. Headlights. "Did you hit me with your car?" The question just came out.

Melinda winced. "Well, almost," she said, not looking at my face. At least she was honest. Her aura was a big swirling mess of colors. "I was driving, and you appeared out of nowhere. You know standing in the middle of the road isn't good for your health. Thank goodness for my swift reflexes. I missed you."

Barely.

I touched my head where there was a small band-aid at my temple. The blue and yellow around her dimmed with remorse. At least she was honest. "My head says otherwise," I said in some humor, though I sounded more morose. Hell, at least I could laugh at what happened instead of cementing myself in anger. Hell, I could be six feet under.

I studied Melinda. She was beautiful, but the dark circle under her eyes said much. Stress? Lack of sleep? I knew how she was feeling.

She took a cautionary step closer. Her eyes roved over my body, then to my face. She looked at me with a finite amount of inspection. "At least, Mr. Bishop, you don't look injured. Thank God for that. Anyway, what were you doing standing in the road in the middle of nowhere Tennessee?"

"I saw…" I wasn't sure how to answer her. I could say a boy, but I wasn't sure I saw him. It could have been another trick of my imagination. Between the spooky woods and the way I was feeling, my subconscious could have conjured up anything.

"What? What did you see?" She folded her hands together and waited.

"I saw your headlights, and the next thing I knew, I woke up here. Why didn't you take me to the hospital?" My irritation kicked in a little as she started to frown.

"You told me not to. You were insistent on it. So I couldn't leave you there in the woods all by yourself, and you didn't want to go to the clinic, so I brought you to my place, even though I think I'm crazy for bringing a stranger into my home, but I felt guilty for nearly hitting you even though it's your fault. Darn it. I'm babbling again. Sorry. I do that when I'm nervous." Melinda's hands bunched tighter, worrying her knuckles to white. "You aren't some crazy psycho killer, are you, Mr. Bishop?"

I almost let out a chuckle at the question. And what was with the formalities. However, it wasn't ridiculous to answer the first part. I shook my head. "No. I'm not a crazy psycho killer. And thank you for not leaving me on the side of the road. You can call me Chase."

"You're welcome, Chase," she chirped, her voice lightened, like the colors around her. Bright and vivid. "I am sorry you got hurt though," she said with slight regret, pointing to the side of my head. "How's your head? I put a band-aid on your temple, but I really think you should go to the clinic today to get checked out."

What I should do was leave. I didn't have time for all this. I had a few more days before the time and date on the back of that card came into play. I wanted to contact the person on this card, and sitting around here wasn't going to get me answers.

"I think I should go. Thanks for letting me crash here. Um…no pun attended."

She let out a relieved chuckle. "I don't think that's a good idea. You're hurt. I'll feel better if you're not walking around with brain damage on my account. So please.'"

My fingers grazed over a bump on the side of my skull. A light fissure of pain radiated out through the tips of my short blond hair.

"Maybe you're right."

"You did hit your head on the ground pretty good. Do you want some aspirin or something for the pain until I take you to the clinic?" From the way she was chewing on her lower lip, I guessed Melinda was getting nervous again. Why? Was she thinking I was going to press charges? Under normal circumstances, I would have bitched up the storm. But currently, I was far from home and not with the dire circumstances I was in.

"Please, a couple of Motrin, if you have it. And my clothes."

"I'll get you the Motrin, and your clothes were dirty, so I washed them. They're in the dryer now. Why don't you go wash up? I'm sure your clothes will be done by the time you're done eating."

"Umm. Thanks. But I'm not hungry. I'll just grab some clothes in my backpack."

"Backpack?" Her eyebrows knitted tight.

"Yes, my backpack."

"I didn't see any bag when I helped you off the ground and into my car last night. Maybe later, we can go back and find it, okay?" she said with a shrug. "It's the least I can do. And my mamma always did say, a head injury deserves a couple of eggs."

"That doesn't make sense."

"Sure it does. That's what my mamma always said. What she said always worked." She shrugged again and stepped out into the hallway. "Well, the bathroom is over there, and I left a new toothbrush on the sink."She then spun around and headed in the opposite direction without another word. So strange.

Needing to take a piss, I headed down the hall in the direction of the bathroom and noticed the walls were littered with pictures. The same happy family adorned the frames, like a shrine. From different seasons to various locations, one thing remained the same throughout. The people in the picture were all smiling. The merriment twinkled in their eyes as though they were truly elated to be with each other. They were Melinda's family. Looking over the faces, a boy in the pictures looked familiar, but I kept trailing my eyes to the other frame images until I reached the last one.

Running a finger over the glass of a picturesque Christmas image in front of a giant Christmas tree, sorrow bubbled up in me. This sudden pang of jealousy raked over me like hot coals, which I instantly squashed it down.

What the fuck was wrong with me? I had no right to feel the way I did. I missed my sister, but looking back; there was nothing to miss in my family.

My father changed for the worst, like something dark twisted up inside the man and took root. He became our worst nightmare. I was so glad that asshole died. I just regretted never finding out what happened to my mother or how she died because my bastard of a father never told us.

Granted, I missed that small part of my life I had long ago buried. There was a time in my life where we were happy. My mother, sister, and even my asshole father were tolerable. Nothing was wrong with the world. Then came reality crashing down on us and everything I loved was gone now. I was alone.

If I had to frame up pictures of my family, it would be only three images. One of Cassie and me during Christmas, the year before our mother died. A high school graduation photo of Cassie and one of our mother sitting by a lake. She was eighteen at the time. Those precious moments were gone now. My family pictures were left back at the apartment where I left Cassie's lifeless body.

MELINDA

Shaking off the nervous butterflies in my stomach, I focused on making breakfast. I heard the shower go on, and I suddenly had an urge to see if he needed an extra towel.

Stay put. I scolded myself.

I flipped the bacon and made some toast. Not long after, Chase entered the kitchen, his nose up as though he was scenting the air. "That smells delicious," he said, his dark blond hair still damp from the shower.

Instead of answering him, I had my tongue hanging out of my mouth as I watched Chase walk out with no shirt on, showing off his sexy six-pack abs and luscious chest. Every inch of Chase's upper torso was exposed for my viewing pleasure. The man had my mind racing with sinful thoughts. I had a sudden urge to lick him like an ice cream cone. It took everything in me to keep my jaw from dropping wider. How could a man be even more gorgeous after he got out of the shower?

I wasn't into guys with closely cropped messy hair, but Chase wore it well.

There was a beat of awkward silence between us when he caught me gawking at his chest where his dark pert nipples were begging for a touch.

"Food ready?" he asked, drawing me out of my lust-induced fog.

"Umm. You hungry?" I asked, looking away from his seductive body. Then it hit me what he asked. "Yes. Almost. How do you like your eggs?"

"Don't go through the trouble. Toast is fine." Chase's smile was shy, but there was a level of strength shown in his light green eyes as he cast a look at the island where there was bacon, homemade biscuits, sausage gravy, and sausage links. He cleared his throat. "You know you didn't have to do all this."

"Yes, I did. I'm a southern girl and my mamma taught me right. Now sit, and how do you like your eggs," I gently ordered, pointing to the chair nearest to Chase. Even though it would be a wonderful sight to behold to eat and stare at him at the same time, the last thing I wanted for this guy was to think I was some mindless hussy, drooling at his naked chest.

Get it together, Melinda.

A buzzer sounded off. "Right on time. Your clothes are done. Oh by the way, I charged your phone." I placed it on the counter.

"Thanks. Now direct me the way to the laundry room."

I pointed toward the other end of the kitchen with some disappointment. "Just through that door."

Not wasting any more time, Chase entered the laundry room and closed the door. I assumed he would change inside there, and I was right when he didn't come out right away. Then I noticed his wallet at the far end of the counter. It never dawned on me to snoop through it, but I wasn't that kind of woman to be nosy, especially with a person's things. Yet, what could it hurt? I didn't know Chase at all.

It was your idea to bring him into your family's home. Sometimes I wanted to smack my annoying inner voice.

Knowing I had only a few seconds, I scanned inside the wallet and froze, staring down at the card I swore I destroyed a couple of weeks ago. My jaw hurt from how hard I clenched my teeth. Where did Chase get this card? Was he working for Randal? God, I hoped not. If he did, he had a rude awakening once he found out that Randal was dead.

I took a closer look at his driver's license. "Hmm. Pennsylvania." Sounds coming from the laundry room had me moving fast. I dropped the wallet, shoved the card in my pocket, and resumed my position in front of the stove. I foolishly assumed Chase looked harmless. Now, I wasn't so sure.

My heart was thumping fast as my anger rushed through my veins. I remained quiet while I heard Chase rustling around in the laundry room.

"Thanks," he said as he opened the door.

"Feel better?" I asked as he stepped back into the kitchen. I barely contained my nervous irritation, but I swallowed it down and began breaking some eggs in the frying pan. We didn't exchange words. I kept my eyes on what I was doing, my back to Chase.

Once I was done cooking, I put the fluffy eggs on a plate and placed them on the table. "You never said what kind of eggs you wanted, so I figure scrambled is safe."

"Yeah. Thanks. Are you okay?" Chase asked, his eyes unblinking as he watched me moved around the kitchen.

"I'm good. Why?" I lied. There was no way I was going to broach the topic of the card right now. My mother always said a man is amendable with a full stomach. Although, the card felt like a lead weight in the pocket of my jeans.

Chase sat and took in our surroundings as though he was looking for something. I did too. White kitchen, with soft touches of powdered blue. Nothing special to the likes of Chase, but for me? It was cute and homey, and it reminded me of my mother.

Then my eyes went to my sparse living room. So what if I hardly had furniture. It was clean and livable. Then my gaze wandered to the old small brown sectional where my family gathered for movie nights and a recliner that my father fell asleep in countless times. I had to swallow down the pain of missing them.

Those last few days I had with them were precious

before a drunk driver took them from me. Even after two years, the hollowness in my chest would never be filled.

A low murmur coming from a flat-screen television was a newly required addition. I had the national weather channel on, which my mother used to watch when she cooked. I didn't know why and we never questioned it.

My eyes swung to the screen, where a weather reporter was standing in the cold rain, right outside a business. The sign overhead read Donovan's Second Hand Shop.

Out of the corner of my eye, Chase's back snapped straight, his green eyes glued to the television. I couldn't decipher what the reporter was saying because the volume was too low, but I can see Chase looked upset.

"Do you mind if I raise the volume on your tv?" he asked, his attention bounced back to the flat screen then to me.

"Sure." My curiosity peaked. As he took the remote and raised the sound a few levels, the broadcast switched to a storm out in Atlanta, Georgia.

"Damn it," he spat out, rubbing the back of his neck. The veins in his neck popped out, and his skin flushed red while a faraway look skimmed his eyes.

I couldn't stay silent anymore. I had to find out what Chase was doing here, especially with my fake business Randal made up. "What's going on, Mr. Bishop?"

That question must have taken his attention to the present because he sat back down and began to eat like nothing happened seconds before. "I just wanted to know what the man was saying about the storm."

His lie came easy, like he was used to doing it all the time. But I could see it clearly. I almost believed him. Almost.

"Don't lie to me, Mr. Bishop." A flash of something I wasn't sure what crossed his beautiful green eyes. Guilt maybe. "Are you wanted by the cops?"

"No," he replied right away, but there was trepidation solid in his voice. "Why do you call me that?"

"Call you what?" I was confused at his question.

"Mr. Bishop. I'm not my father. Just call me Chase."

"What kind of trouble are you in, Chase?" To the point questions weren't like me, but I had to ask. Then I rounded the kitchen table and stood across from him. I grabbed his wallet and dropped it on the whitewashed oak table with the business card between my fingers. "Then explain to me why and where did you get my card?"

4

CHASE

S hock tore through me at her declaration. "You're the Melinda Bradley?"

"That is my name," she huffed out, her eyes averted mine. "Now, tell me, where did you get this card. And by the way, it's fake."

"What do you mean fake? That doesn't make any sense." I tried to temper my voice, but it was hard controlling my emotions. Since I didn't know Melinda, and there's so much on the line, I wasn't sure if I should spill the truth or hold back.

Jesus, this whole time, she was the one I was looking for. And so fucking coincidental that she was the one who almost ran me over.

"You have to be honest with me, Chase." Her voice shook with trepidation. "Why do you have this card?— what's going on with you?"

Honesty had limits. I, of all people knew that. Trust came with a price, and I lost too much already trusting John with Cassie. I didn't know Melinda at all to give her my trust. Hell, it took me several years to entrust John, and he'd been a part of my life for a hell of a lot longer. How do I trust Melinda when I didn't know a thing about her?

Granted, she took me in when she didn't have to. Melinda could have easily left me on the side of that road. But she didn't. She brought me into her home, cleaned me up, and was feeding me.

I mean, I could trust her with some details—but not about Cassie's murder—not yet. With whatever composure I had left, my eyes went to Melinda. I picked up my fork and asked, "What do you want to know?"

"Where did you find the card? Why were you so interested in that particular news? What are you hiding? And why in God's name were you standing in the middle of the road last night in the middle of nowhere? Are you some maniac?" Her voice cracked at the last question.

I wanted to laugh at the last question she spat out but i held my resolve.

"If I were a maniac, I wouldn't be sitting here eating breakfast with you," I chastised. "I'm not here to kill you or anyone else. You can relax," I said with another scoop of eggs.

Melinda's shoulders slumped a bit, but it wasn't much. And I didn't stop her from whipping the card at me either. "Start talking, Chase Bishop, or I'm going to make a call to the sheriff's office." That when I noticed a cell phone clutched in Melinda's hand. Her harsh don't-fuck-with-me glare was proof of her impatience and fear that she was right on her promise. That was warning enough for me.

I don't blame her. Melinda didn't know me, but then why did she bring me here? I shoved that thought aside and tried to keep down the acrid burn at the back of my throat from coming up. I placed my fork down on the plate and swallowing the egg, which tasted like ash in my mouth.

"Please sit down, and I'll explain. Please." The plea sounded reasonable, but I was far from it. My insides twisted in knots at the thought of telling this absolute stranger of my sister's murder, and I was following this card as a lead to catch her killer.

I picked up the card and turned it over to the back, where the date, time, and place were written in chicken scratch handwriting.

"Where did you get that card?" Melinda softly repeated as she took a seat on the other side of the kitchen table. She was ramrod stiff, her hands on the tabletop, with the cell phone ready.

"I found the card with my sister—that's the truth—I swear." Anger receded, and regret was in its place. The festering pain in my heart was brewing, but I pushed on. "That's why I'm here. My sister Cassie was murdered eight days ago, and the only clue is this card. See this?" I pointed to the words. "Whoever killed my sister will be here at this time and date. I know it."

I grabbed my wallet and pulled the only current picture of Cassie out of the plastic protector. I slid the small high school grad picture of my sister to Melinda. "This is my sister. She had ASD."

Grief seeped out of my pores, choking me with every inhale. Melinda picked up the photo and shook her head. "I'm sorry." She slid it back to me. "But I don't know her," she said, her blue eyes filled with tears. "I know firsthand what it feels like to lose loved ones, especially to murder." The muted blue magnified around her aura, and deep sorrow filtered into the room.

"I'm sorry too." I meant it. No one should go through a loss like that. I wanted to reach out for her hand that lay loosely on the table, but I felt she would retract from my touch.

What I said was the truth, and maybe...

"Melinda, I need your help. Whoever had this card has the answers to my sister's death. Either they killed her, or they know who did it."

Melinda shook her head. She pointed to it as though it was evil. "I told you this card is fake."

"What do you mean fake?" My eyes narrowed on the card and then to her face, which was pinched with anger. She stared down at the card, her eyes intent like she wanted it to burn up right there.

"I'm mean, it's not real. The person who made up the cards thought he could force me to work for his real estate company by creating these." She slapped her hand down over the card. The impact rattled the small ceramic rooster fruit bowl in the center of the table. "Sorry. Thinking of that man makes me want to punch something."

"So you're not a real estate agent?" I was thoroughly confused.

"Yes, I am, but not with Dark Hollow Lake Reality. I'll be starting my own agency next month—but at the time these cards were made—I wasn't. But that's not the point. This card is a lie. I never worked for J. Randal or his company."

"What does J stand for?" I knew it was a stupid question to ask, but I was curious.

"His first name is James. But Randal liked to act like a big man and wanted only to be called by his last name. How ridiculous was that?"

"Where is this J. Randal?" I picked up the fake business card and stared at the detail inscribed on the front. The idea that this James Randal was connected to

Cassie's murder brought some hope that I was heading in the right direction and that getting almost killed by Melinda could have been fate.

"That no-good swindling narcissistic jerk is dead." She expelled an exasperated breath. "God, I thought I burned all those cards."

"What do you mean dead?" Not wanting her words to be valid.

"Randal is dead. About two and a half weeks ago. I think that Thursday. He broke his neck when he fell down the stairs at his office. I remember that day well." Her pinched expression morphed into a subtle but implacable smile. "Karma can be a mean one, you know."

The dread wheedled in, squashing any ideas of confronting this J. Randal. Then a thought hit me like a sledgehammer. "You said you burned the cards? When?"

"That Wednesday, the day before Randal fell. The box was sitting on his desk when I saw it. I was so pissed, I took them and burned the entire box that same day. Or so I thought. Why?"

"My sister was murdered eight days ago, which makes it about a week after Randal's death." The spark of that information lit my insides. Whoever killed Cassie had to have known J. Randal.

"I'm not getting it." Melinda was chewing her lower lip. The yellow in her aura dulled.

"It means someone who knew Randal took one of your cards when he was alive—"

"Those aren't my cards," she shot out. "I have no affiliation with that bastard." The grit in Melinda's tone conveyed without a doubt she hated the man. If a man was so hated, maybe his fall wasn't an accident. What if the man was pushed down the stairs? My eyes strayed to Melinda.

Could she? Would she? No. I would have seen it in her aura. I would have also sensed the negative energy around her. No. She was no more a killer than I was.

"Chase, where did you go?" The wave of her hand in my face jarred me out of my thoughts. "Are you all right?"

"Sorry. Bad habit." I didn't explain further. Instead, I stood and started to pace. The movements helped me to think while Melinda watched me studiously from her seat. "Whoever took that card was in my house and killed my sister." My whole body was vibrating with excitement. I was a step closer to finding out who murdered Cassie. Albeit a small one, but still a step.

I should call John, but this new detail was only one piece of the puzzle. I needed more proof.

"Melinda, I know I'm asking a lot, and you don't know me, but can you help me? I have no one here." Trepidation and concern shadowed her face and aura. Melinda took a few long silent moments, where I held my breath for her answer.

"Yes. Depends on what do you need me to do."

Tension eased from my body as I thought for a second how Melinda could help. "Can you make me a list of Mr. Randal's friends and the people he had pissed off?" I didn't know it was a challenging request, but the look of consternation on Melinda's face had me asking, "Did I say something wrong?"

"I wouldn't know where to begin." The snippet of indignation in her tone made Melinda's cheeks blush redder. It was almost cute. "There are many who didn't like the man."

"That list could be important to narrow down the

suspects. And maybe his office could hold some clues. I don't know what but," I picked up the card, turned to where the date and time showed. "This is important. We can look on his calendar to see if any of his future meetings would match the time, date, and place."

Melinda took the card and studied the writing. "I agree, but first things first. It would be best if you went to the clinic and get checked out. I would feel better that you got a clean bill of health first. At least for my sanity sake."

"It's not necessary. I'm fine."

"Fine only works in caster sugar," Melinda said with a grin but quickly faltered. "It's what my mother used to say before she—never mind." Melinda averted her eyes, grabbed her purse, and headed out the door. I wasn't sure what she meant, but I couldn't mistake the heart-wrenching sadness that reflected in her eyes or the sorrowful muted blue seeping into her aura.

5

CHASE

Not even down half of a block from her house, I turned to Melinda, determined to see the dead realtor's office first. There had to be some clues to who was behind Cassie's murder, mostly while everything from that night was still fresh in my head.

"Before we go to the clinic, I want to see Randal's office first hand. I have a feeling some of the answers I'm looking for are there. And I have this feeling that Randal's death wasn't an accident."

"Really? I never thought that someone would want to kill the man. But, Chase, I don't think that is a good idea." A note of hesitation in her voice when mentioning Randal's office was clear cut. She didn't like the place.

"Why?" I belt out the word with a bit more gruffness than I wanted to. I was getting agitated, but I refused to let it control me. The way Melinda bit her lower lip, I knew she was hiding something. "What aren't you telling me?"

She quickly looked at me and then back to the road, eyes pinched at the corners. "I don't feel comfortable talking about it or being in there. The place gives me the creeps."

"Then I'll go in there by myself. You can stay in the car." I thought my solution was concrete. But she shook her head no. "Why not?"

"A few days after Randal died, I got a call from his widow, Kathy. She wanted to meet up at the office to oversee some of his things that were pertinent to me. I didn't want to go, but Kathy assured me that she doesn't want anything to do with the business and is willing to hand over the office space and most of the contents inside it to me for free. So I agreed to meet her there. However, when I got there, which happened to be about ten minutes early than Kathy asked—you know I hate being late and—"

"Get to the point, Melinda," I blurted out but instantly regretted it when her blue eyes narrowed at me, and her lips thinned into a frown. "Sorry. Please continue."

She lost some of her frown. With pursed lips, she said, "It's all right. I have a bad habit of rambling when I'm nervous." Melinda snapped her mouth shut.

"So you keep saying. Now, what happened when you got there?" I urged, wanting the details out of her mouth.

She let out a resolute breath. "When I got there, the front door was unlocked and the place was dark. Which was weird because Kathy told me that she was going to do some paperwork in the back office and to knock."

"Did you?"

"I did, but I tried the door first, which I found it unlocked. I went inside, and the place looked the same when I last saw it. I didn't think much of it when I started walking toward the back office, assuming Kathy forgot to turn on the lights." Melinda swallowed hard; a glimmer of fear flashed in her eyes. "I was about to head upstairs after checking the back office, I assumed she might be in second floor office. I called her name and thought I saw someone standing at the top of the staircase. When I looked up, there was nobody there. Then an ice-cold chill came over me like someone dumped ice water over my head. The creepiest thing that happened was that I smelled Randal's god-awful cologne. With that, I had to get out of there. With or without talking to Kathy."

"Whatever happened to Kathy?" I asked with curiosity.

"She was running late that day and left me a message that she was going to be an hour later than what she said. Funny thing was that for some reason, I never got the message. Anyway, I ended up meeting with her later that day at the Dark Hollow Pastries, where she handed me the keys to the building and told me good luck."

"Chase, I can't be too sure, but I think James Randal is haunting that building. Most people don't believe in ghosts, but I'm not one of them." With the earnest tone Melinda evoked, I had to take her opinion seriously.

"Noted. But I still need to see and check for myself."

"Then I'll stay here while you go look. I can't say I didn't warn you. Now, I'm only giving you ten minutes before I come to the door and shout for you, or if I lose my nerve, I'll call the sheriff, and he can get your butt out of that building."

I laugh, but her frown meant business.

"I understand. Ten minutes."

We pulled up to an ordinary brick building with a typical-looking reality marquee that hung above the door. The housing availability were displayed in the bay window were just as expected. I glanced over to

Melinda, who was chewing on her lower lip so much that she'd eventually chew through her lip and a pinprick of blood eked out. Not realizing it, I reached over and touched her chin. "You're going to chew your lip until there's nothing left. Relax. I'm not afraid of any ghost, if there's one inside. Promise."

That one touch made Melinda's eyes widen. Wasn't sure if she was freaked that I mentioning ghost or that my finger skimmed along her jawline. A spark from that touch did something to me too, but I said nothing.

She pulled back slightly, keeping herself a finger length away. "Please, be careful. And add my number to your phone, just in case you need me. I can't say if I'd come, but—"

"Melinda." The whisper of her name clamped her mouth shut. "Thanks. But I don't think I'll need your help." I gave her one last reassuring look before adding her cell phone to my phone and climbed out of the car.

"Chase," Melinda called out as she lowered the passenger side window all the way. "The keys."

I snagged the keys out of the air and sent her a quick smile of thanks. Keys in hand, I unlocked the front door and walked into the reception area with purpose. My eyes wandered around the room, and noticed a thin layer of dust along the tabletop and furniture. I listened for any odd noise or sounds that didn't fit with the silence of the space.

A slight tick from the vents was the only thing I heard as I passed the front desk and into a short hallway that opened up to two other offices and a staircase that led to the second floor. That must have been where Melinda felt something.

I walked over to the bottom steps, staring up to the second floor. There, at the top of the landing, stood a man barely containing his anger. He had the same grey paler as the boy, the colors of his aura were dark— mostly black around him.

Before I got a chance to move, he shouted something that sounded muted to my ears and hurled himself toward me.

"James Randal!" I shouted, my heart beating out of my chest. It was a second before I moved out of the way as he landed in a heap by my feet. The look of surprise and then emptiness filled his black eyes before Randal disappeared altogether like smoke and magic. My heart all but jumped out of my chest as I stood there, not believing what I was seeing.

Melinda was right.

Yet, ghost or not, nothing or no one was going to stop me from looking around. I headed up the stairs and quickly checked every room. The first room was crowded with old office furniture, and I knew I wouldn't find anything useful. I checked the second room, which was set up as a genuine office. I searched through a desk that had piles of old transactions of sales from the past several years.

The final room was a messy bedroom, which surprised me. Either Randal didn't live at home, or someone else was bunking in here. I needed to ask Melinda about it.

I went through the drawers and skimmed the area before I decided there was nothing viable I could use. Right before I stepped out of the room, I heard footsteps coming up the stairs. Looking around the room, I spotted a baseball bat and immediately grabbed it. Ready with the weapon, I waited until I saw a shadow in my sights.

I jumped out, ready to swing the wood weapon, when Melinda screamed out in horror.

"Dang it, Chase, you scared the crap out of me." She clutched at her chest, breathing ragged from the scare, eyes wildly looking around her.

"Sorry. I didn't expect to see you in here," I said, dropping the bat to my side.

"You were taking so long. So I drew up my courage and came in here to search for you. What are you doing?" Melinda questioned through quick expelled breaths. "Did you find anything?"

"No. Nothing that connects Randal to Cassie."

"Did... you see anything... odd?" she asked with a deep swallow that I could see her pulse jumping on her neck.

I knew what she was asking, but what was the point in telling her about Randal's ghost. I didn't want to frighten her anymore. "No. Nothing out of the ordinary."

She eyed me warily before dropping the topic. "Let's get out of here and get you to the clinic."

"All right." I leaned the bat on the door frame but changed my mind and took it with me. I followed Melinda out of the building. "Hey, got a question."

"Shoot," she said as she got into her car.

"Was Randal and Kathy separated that he'd be sleeping here?"

She cutely wrinkled her nose before answering. "Not that I'm aware of. And there's no gossip about any impending break-up between the two. Why?"

"The last room upstairs was a bedroom, and it looks like someone has recently slept there. I wonder if Randal has late nights and crashes there instead of going home."

"Not that I'm aware of. How lived in is it? Because no one is allowed in that building without my permission since the business is officially mine now."

"I'm sure not for a little while, but I can't be correct,"

I admitted with a smile that seemed to ease the tension out of Melinda's shoulders. Truth was, it looked like someone slept in the bed last night because the cigarette smell in the room was much sharper, opposed to someone lit up a few weeks ago. "I'm sure there's nothing to worry about."

"I hope you're right," Melinda drawled out before she pulled away from the curb.

Me too.

6

CHASE

B elieve it or not, Melinda was more than helpful
than I wanted to admit. On the short ride to the
clinic, she explained a little bit about herself, the town of
Dark Hollow Lake, and the people in this town.

Born and raised in Dark Hollow Lake, Melinda knew
practically everyone in town and most in the surrounding
area. From the Mayor to the postal worker that had been
delivering her mail since she could remember. Dark
Hollow Lake was a small knitted community getting into
everyone's business—her words—not mine.

"As an agent, I've been keeping up with the progress
of this town and the surrounding areas. I know who
moved in and out of town and in the surrounding area in
the last few years. I'm sure with a few phone calls, I can
dig around on a solid list of Randal's possible enemies
and possibly Cassie's killer."

"Thank you. I'd appreciate that," I said evenly, but
my insides tightened from apprehension. I hoped that it
was enough to lead me straight to who murdered my

sister. However, I still had few days left to the date
written on the card.

We pulled up to the older brick building nestled
between a quaint veterinary office and a hardware store.
The clinic was just that—a clinic. Stepping past the
double doors, an astringent odor like disinfectant
lingered in the air. It made my nose twitch. We were met
with a non-sterile bright baby blue reception area, a
significant contrast to what I was smelling.

"Melinda, what a surprise to see you. Is everything
okay?" A young man in his early twenties asked as
concern laced his voice. The bright orange, yellow, and
red aura that surrounded him contradicted what his face
conveyed.

"No, Peter. I'm not here for me. I want Dr. Cooper to
look over my friend Chase." Melinda nodded toward me.
Her face conveyed some of that remorse as her shoulder
slumped at her unspoken words to me. Jesus, we needed
to have words with her apologies.

"We had a bit of an accident last night, and I want to
make sure he's okay." A bit of an accident? That annoyed
me a bit, but I kept my mouth shut.

"Sure. Give me a minute to sort out Kinsley's boy."
He looked over at me, and a small shot of annoyance
puffed out between his lips before he pasted on a slight
smile that didn't quite reach his brown eyes. Those vivid
colors shifted from vibrant to slightly dull. Worry. Yet,
he didn't say anything.

"What did Rette do now?" A soft note of concern
came through Melinda's question, but the light-hearted
chuckle soon followed had me thinking that this Rette
went in a lot.

"He stuck one of Kinsley's decorating tools—you
know the one that has a ball at each end to make edible

flowers—Anyway, Rette stuck one side up to his nose, and it got lodged inside too tight that Kinsley couldn't pull it out."

"Oh my." Melinda's blue eyes sparked with humorous concern.

"Don't worry, Doc Cooper will dislodge it. Maybe it'll give that boy an idea not to shove something up his nose except for his fingers." Peter then shivered with disgust.

The amusement lit on Melinda's face, which turned infectious. She turned to me, smiling huge, and I couldn't help but grin back at her, even though my nerves seemed exposed. I could get used to that smile every day. But I quickly shut that shit down before the idea dug in.

I haven't felt like laughing for a long time, and here I was doing just that. Even not knowing what was going on at John's end of Cassie's case, the laughter eased some of the heaviness I've been carrying. Not knowing was still a burden on me, but in this moment I was enjoying every second being here with her.

"Rette is seven years old and tends to get into mischief now and then." Melinda's voice brought me out of my thoughts.

"Now and then? That kid will lose a limb by the time he turns eight if he keeps this up," Peter retorted with a snort of laughter. His brown eyes pointed to me. "I need you to fill this out..." His words dropped off when Melinda shook her head.

"Can we keep this on the down-low?" Her pursed lips and the seriousness in her eyes must have convinced Peter, because he looked at me with curiosity instead of dislike and gave her a slow nod. I wondered at this moment if Melinda tended to hit people with her car more often than she admitted. That ridiculous thought made me inwardly chuckle.

"He still needs to fill this out so Dr. Cooper will know what to look for." He handed me a clipboard and pen. "Have a seat, and I'll get Dr. Cooper as soon as she's done." Peter scurried past a set of doors to the left.

I glanced down at the sheet where they wanted my personal information. The pen point hovered millimeters above the title labeled name and address.

"Don't worry. Let's put in my home address," she said as she took the seat next to me and leaned toward me.

I wasn't going to argue with her. So I nodded, which she promptly rattled off the address.

"Thanks."

"Thanks, but not needed. I hit you remember?" Melinda turned away from me, picked up a gossip magazine on the side table, and skimmed through the pages. "Besides, you want to be healthy if you have to track down your sister's killer," she whispered out the truth.

She was right about that.

It wasn't long before Peter directed us to a small room with a curtain for a door. The space was no bigger than a large walk-in closet. "Dr. Cooper will be right in. Melinda, can I have a word with you in private?" The tension in Peter's voice was noted, along with a swirl of weary colors around him.

"Sure," she said with furrowed brows. Just before Melinda stepped out of the room, she turned to me. "I'll be out in the waiting room and start making that list?" She winked and walked away.

"Sounds good," I called out to her, and before I could tell her to stay, Peter quickly closed the curtain on me. Little shit. What happened to small-town hospitality?

Five minutes went by before a beautiful dark skinned woman drew back the curtain. "Hello, I'm Dr. Cooper. You are... Chase?" There was no drawl from this woman. Bright colors surrounded her, which exuded warmth and kindness.

"You're not from here," I said bluntly.

"No. I'm from Chicago. Why?" she asked, her dark chocolate eyes studied me.

"Just surprised, I guessed." I shrugged. "I thought you'd be a local."

"Well, I'm a local now. I've been a part of this town for ten years. Do you want my proof of residency, or should I check to see what's wrong with you first?" Her snarky attitude made me smile.

"No need for the proof, and I would appreciate the check-up," I admit somewhat sheepishly.

"Well, you don't look sick," she said as her eyes accessed me from head to foot.

"Aside from the bump on the side of my head, I'm good, Doc."

"Let me be the judge of that. Headaches? Nausea? Any vomiting? Dizziness?" The gravity of her tone was meant to be abided.

"A slight headache. No nausea or vomiting, but I was slightly dizzy when I woke up this morning."

"How did you get that bump on your head?" she asked as she put on gloves. The indigo and sharp blue of her aura calmed me as she began examination.

This was going to be embarrassing. "Melinda hit me with her car."

Her wide eyes shot to my face, and her mouth dropped partially open. "Are you serious?"

"I am, but it no big deal. I'm fine. There is no

damage," I said with nonchalance, hoping it lessened the worry across the doctor's furrowed brows.

"Alrighty then," Dr. Cooper muttered and went on examining me.

MELINDA

"Who is that guy?" Peter dragged me back into the reception area. "Is he your boyfriend?" A slight pink tinged his cheeks when he asked. "I mean, I've never seen him around town."

"No. Chase is a guy I... um, he's a friend." I wasn't sure if I should confess about hitting him with my car. "Chase is a friend who got hurt. That's all you need to know, nosy Peter." I bopped him on his nose with my pointy finger.

"Ms. Melinda Bradley, may I have a word with you in private?" The cutting question to my right had me facing off with one and only Mrs. Marion Whitlow. She was one of the founding families that established Dark Hollow Lake, but was meaner than a rattler.

I turned my attention to the brash woman, who was staring at me with daggers in her eyes. Donned in heavy makeup, dressed in black slacks, a long cashmere blazer, short heeled shoes that probably worth more than my salary and Chanel number five was clogging the air space.

Marion Whitlow was usually a recluse, hardly talked to anyone—far from having a pleasant and friendly manner—or any manners at. But she was a force to be reckoned with, especially when she was in a snit. Her abrupt, rude, and insensitive manner was like a wrecking ball.

I had firsthand dealing with her two years back, during my family's funeral. I had been highly emotional when she walked into the funeral home and started a fuss. I didn't care if she was a founding member of our town or not. She rubbed me the wrong way the instant she opened her mouth and had started bad-mouthing my mother. Trust me, it wasn't a pleasant experience telling her to leave that day.

"Excuse me, Peter." I walked over to the older woman, my mouth tight with annoyance. "What can I do for you, Mrs. Whitlow?" I said as cordially I could muster up for this terrible woman.

Killer her with your kindness my mamma would say.

"Who is that man you walked in with?" She lashed out the words like it was an actual slap.

I narrowed my eyes on her. I wasn't going to give in to her demands. "Why?"

"That is none of your concern. Just answer my question, girlie," she said as her eyes were like a hawk on the door that led to the examining rooms. God, I hated being called that.

I crossed my arms and stared at Marion. I hardly knew Chase, but I'd be damned if I let this woman loose on him. Not without information first to defend himself.

"I'm waiting," I said evenly. I wouldn't let my irritation get the better of me. Not like the last time. "Why?"

"You're just like your mother. Obstinate," she huffed out.

"Thank you." She didn't like my response. But I didn't waver either.

"Fine." Her thin shoulders straightened back even

more. "That man you walked in with is my grandson. I have the right to know what happened to him." Her tone settled as her eyes wavered back to the empty doorway and then to me. The crestfallen expression on her face surprised me in a way that I wanted to reach out to steady myself against the wall, but I stayed firm where I stood.

"Mrs. Whitlow, Chase isn't from Dark Hollow Lake. He can't be your grandson." Delusional old bat. "There's no resemblance."

"Don't patronize me, girlie. I know who my grandson is." There was that whip again.

"Mrs. Whitlow, I don't know if that is true, but I'm sure we can figure this out once Chase is finished with Dr. Cooper and comes out."

"Figure what out?" I jumped at Chase's voice. He approached us; his attention fixed on Marion. He then looked at me, a silent question of what's going on conveyed in his brilliant green eyes.

"Chase, this is Mrs. Marion Whitlow. She thinks—"

"I don't think, girlie. I know Chase Bishop is my grandson."

7

CHASE

"I'm your what?" At the same time, Melinda asked how this Marion Whitlow knew my name. I wasn't sure if I heard the old woman correctly and repeated, "I'm your what?"

I stared at the woman as I took in her white hair primed in place with a thick layer of hairspray. Marion had some notable amount of makeup and expensive clothes I used to see in some windows off the Mag Mile in Chicago when I had a load to drop off in the windy city. The deep creases between her brown penciled eyebrows marred her face with more wrinkles. However, the moment I stare into her cornflower blue eyes—the same color as Cassie's, a spark of recognition shadowed my memory. It took me back a bit, but then something lit my attention. Her aura flashed in and out like a light switch flipping on and off from muted shades of grays and the brilliance of multiple hues. I've never seen anyone's aura do that before.

"You heard me." Her words pulled me out of my thought. "Don't act stupid, boy." The disapproval in her tone felt like a slap across the face. "This isn't the place or time to discuss this. I'll take care of the bill. You wait for me outside." Like a piece of lint, she flicked me off with a wave of the hand and sauntered to the front desk.

Stunned at the hard, no-nonsense of Marion Whitlow, I turned and did as she commanded. Melinda followed right behind me.

"Did you know that she's my grandmother?" I asked Melinda, but she was too speechless to respond. I didn't give a shit one way or another, but I had to know if she kept this from me. "Is it true?" I pushed.

"I didn't know. This is the first I heard of it." Eyes still wide, Melinda shook her head. "So she is telling the truth? Marion is your kin?" There was a hint of censure in her voice. "Because that's a shame."

"I have no clue if she is. But she does look familiar to me. Why are—" My words were cut off when the Marion walked out and proclaimed with a wave to me to follow.

"Don't dally," she spurred on.

"I'm—"

"Melinda." The gentleness of Marion Whitlow's voice both surprised Melinda and me that I swore she's bi-polar. "I would like a word with you too. Please, follow behind us," she said as she handed me a set of keys and ordered me to drive.

I wasn't sure if I should laugh or be mad at the way this woman dictated me around like I was her servant. But, my mom taught me right about the elderly, and did what Marion Whitlow bid and did not argue.

Glancing over at Melinda, she stood there stock-still. Eyes to me in what-the-hell attitude on her face. With the spire of red in her aura and a deep frown across her face, she wasn't happy to comply with Marion's request.

I turned back to Marion, watched her slide into the passenger side of a two-door classic 1970 cherry red Oldsmobile Cutlass 442 convertible. The vehicle immediately captured all my attention. What could I say? The car was absolute perfection, and since I was a car nut, I quickly complied.

Still, slightly gobsmacked, I pulled opened the driver side door as though it was made of glass and climbed in. Aside from a single tiny rip in the driver's seat, the car was in pristine condition. I slipped the key into the ignition, turned it, and the engine purred to life. It was manna to my ears.

"Beautiful," I whispered in awe, stroking the steering wheel.

"I know. It belonged to your grandfather. This was Johnny's baby." A small stone lodged in my throat at the sadness and yearning in her voice. All this time, Cassie and I had family, and not at any time did my father or mother ever told us about them. The topic had been voodoo whenever I had asked.

"Why?" The word strained from my throat, but she understood my meaning.

She patted my arm. "I have the answers. We'll talk as soon as you put the car into drive and take me home."

She directed me to the West side of Dark Hollow Lake, where larger, more substantial homes were established. I periodically tracked Melinda's car in my rearview mirror, which remained a few cars' lengths back.

"I'm sorry about Cassie." Marion's words knocked the breath out of my lungs before I veered from the road and stopped. I immediately put the car in park and stared at the woman next to me with vehemence.

I swallowed hard, not expecting that news out of her

mouth. Quickly turning my attention back on the road, but my fingers tightened around the steering wheel like it was the murderer's neck that took Cassie's life.

"How did you find out about her death?" I barely got out between clenched teeth.

"I have my ways." I hated her statement. I didn't care if she was my kin. This woman didn't know me. I wanted answers, and apparently, she knew more than what she was letting on.

I twisted, leaning close to her. "Tell me who killed Cassie?" I barked out. She grabbed her chest in shock, her eyes filled with a shot of fear and a whole lot of indignation.

"Control yourself," she bit out. "Don't act like your father."

Her words were a blow to my solar plexus. She knew my father well, and I quickly regretted my irrational outburst. Taking my anger and frustrations out on Marion was inexcusable.

"I'm sorry," I said with regret and pulled myself back into the driver's seat. "It's been a long nine days, and I want answers. That's why I'm in a town. But I never thought I'd meet a woman who says she's my grandmother."

She took out a deep breath and slowly reached out with a shaky hand and touched my right bicep. "I know this will come as a shock, but you have been here before, Chase. Once, a long time ago. And I loved you and your sister for all of your lives. Never forget that."

I eyed the woman and realized inside the shade of the car, Marion Whitlow had dark shadows under her eyes. She looked almost fragile compared to the stringent woman I met only moments before.

"Come on, let's get home, have a good stiff drink,

and I'll tell you everything. Okay?" she said, dropping her hand off my arm and stared out the windshield.

I caught her fragile hand in mine and squeezed, letting her know without words that our meeting like this was huge. The knotted-up emotions inside me were unraveling every mile I drove. This was my grand-mother. Family. Family I could have loved. Could have shared with Cassie. She could have been safe if we knew of Marion.

I felt the tightness in my chest and pinch in my eyes. I wasn't sure who to blame for this fucked up catastrophe call my life. But Marion was here and alive. Not Cassie.

From the way Marion was squeezing my hand, she was also feeling the riot of emotions.

Releasing her hand, I said, "Let's get you back home." Then I put the car into drive and drove toward the directions she dictated.

Several streets passed, she finally pointed to a large two-story brick colonial coming up onto the left. I gawked at the size of the home and the property that surrounded it. The hitch in my breathing wasn't audible, but I swore my heart was beating out of my chest. My grandmother had money. This whole time, she could have helped Cassie, helped me take care of my sister. That knowledge reignited my anger, but I quickly tapped it down. It wasn't Marion's fault how my life turned out. Still.

I pulled onto the driveway, she clicked the garage door remote that was clamped onto the visor three times and opened the three-bay doors of a four-car detached garage. As I put the Olds in park and climbed out of the vehicle, my eyes stay trained on the sixties Mustang in the far-left bay. From what I could see, the car had seen better days. Then there was another vehicle shielded by a grey tarp, but the bulk it was hiding.

Marion pointed to the Mustang. "That too was your grandfather's. But he died before he got a chance to work on it."

"Why did you keep it if it doesn't work?" I asked with a note of wonder.

"Because it was my husband's. I couldn't part with it. Any of them." I felt the deep sadness as her blue gaze focused on the vehicles. A small hint of purple and pink flashed around her but quickly evaporated like a spark.

Marion—my grandmother—went back to study me for a long second like she knew what I was doing. Then it hit me. Did she have the gift to see? As I studied her face, it occurred that this woman standing before me in a calm state was the older version of my mother and of Cassie.

"I know you have the gift too, Chase." It was all Marion said, with a knowing smile spread across her wrinkled face. She walked into the house without another word.

8

CHASE

I wasn't sure if stunned was how I felt at the new revelation. All this time, I thought I was the only one who had the talent of seeing auras. If Marion saw them, I wondered if my mother or even Cassie did too.

After a moment of contemplation, I suddenly realized that Melinda was nowhere in sight. I walked down the end of the driveway, looked both ways down the road for her car. To my disappointment, her vehicle was nowhere to be seen.

"Damn it." I shook my head, irritated by her vanishing act. I drudged out my phone and called her. Four rings in, and I got her voice mail. "Thanks, Melinda for ditching me."

I ended the call with another soft growl. Melinda's avoidance rubbed me the wrong way. Though, who could blame her. Meeting Marion was the last thing I expected, and I was sure back at the clinic, Melinda didn't look happy being around her.

Maybe it was a good thing that Melinda didn't come. I could get to know Marion better without any distractions. And I had come to realize that Melinda was the biggest. With that thought, I headed to the house.

A sense of familiarity scratched at my brain as I looked around the property and then the home. Staring up at the two-story colonial, it felt like de ja vue. Marion was right. I've been here before.

Marion—my grandmother stood in the doorway waiting, impatience marring the corners of her eyes. "That girl has no spine," she claimed, then turned around with a huff into the house.

With the trepidation of my own, I followed her inside and closed the door.

From the pristinely manicured lawn and empty flower beds trimmed around the house, the outside showed a promise of what was to come in the spring. But the inside of the house? It was a whole other matter. Dirty wasn't the word I would use. It was definitely cluttered. Cluttered to the point that it was hard to maneuver around the space without knocking something over. Hoarder was what came to mind.

My grandmother was a hoarder. Mounds of mail were piled by the door, on top of a small round table. Newspapers were stacked several feet high in neat tall rows. Shoe boxes—yes, I did say shoeboxes were lined on the other side. They were layered at least twelve high, reaching the low-hanging chandelier. I wondered what was in those boxes and how in the hell she got them down there without toppling them or herself to the floor.

I had to angle my shoulders sideways not to collapse the makeshift barricades of stuff nearing the doorway she went through.

"Are you coming, Chase, or do I have to send out the dogs?" I had to chuckle. Then I heard a bark ahead of me. Shit, she wasn't kidding.

I hurried my pace until I came to a brightly lit room. Clutter-free. It was a kitchen. Small, with a white table set up for what looked like to me, high tea—without the hats—of course. Different kinds of finger sandwiches sat on doilies plates. Tiny decorated cakes and cookies were situated on plain white china, matching teacups and saucers next to them.

"Having a party?" I asked with some confusion while scanning the small feast.

A loud yip in the corner caught my attention. The second I shifted, a beast of a dog trundled over, his tongue lolling out of his mouth. The Great Dane-Mastiff mix. I didn't know where my knowledge of this dog came from but there it was.

He sat his butt right in front of me and turned his massive head from side to side as though he was studying me just as much as I was looking at him. The black-brown animal was huge and quite intimidating. But the way he yipped and how his eyes kept glancing at the sandwiches, the dog wasn't stupid. He was pleading for a treat.

"Yeager." That name popped into my head.

My grandmother's eye went wide in surprise. "You remember Yeager?"

"I… the name just came to me," I admitted with reservation. The last thing I wanted to sound like was an idiot.

"This is his son Yeager Jr. You used to play with his daddy when your mother brought you around. I bet if Yeager were alive, he would have remembered you too. Yes." She nodded her head as if envisioning the moment. Marion's eyes filled with moister, but she quickly wiped them away and turned to the dog. "You're a good boy, aren't you, baby."

The dog wagged his tail with her positive acknowledgment and a pat on his large head. She then threw Junior a finger sandwich, which he promptly snatched out of the air.

Marion looked back at me with a sad smile. "The last time you were here was right before your grandfather died. It was one momentous day, Chase. I know your grandfather never forgot it, and neither did I." The deep regret in her familiar blues eyes scored me down to the bone. I wished Cassie was here to experience this with me.

I felt the dog's hulking body leaning against my leg. I leaned over and scratched behind the dog's ears before I sat down in the chair Marion pointed to. "I have to be honest. Coming to this town and meeting you are the last thing I expected."

"I can understand that. See, your father... well, you know how your father is."

"Yeah, I know well enough… he's dead now, and I don't have to worry about him anymore."

She looked at me for a second, eyes slightly narrowed like she wanted to say something but remained quiet.

"Please explain to me how you know about Cassie's death," I asked. Exhaustion started to ring out of me everything time Cassie's name and her death was brought up, but I pushed through.

She placed a couple of different kinds of sandwiches on my empty plate. Then gracefully poured me a cup of tea. "I had a dream. She came to me, a warning to look out for danger. And that sweet girl also told me you were coming here. So I watched and waited."

I leaned back against the chair and stared at her in disbelief. "A dream?" My words came out as such like she was crazy. But I quickly recovered and watched a run of emotions skated across my grandmother's face.

"Yes—and don't give me that look, Chase Bishop— I'm telling you the truth. You see. Most people don't believe, but we're proof that the supernatural does exist. Or how this town exists. You have to understand that your mamma's family came from a long line of powerful seers. Seers that for many generations were persecuted for talents to see visions, auras and decipher dreams and even see ghosts. Didn't your mamma ever tell you where your gift came from?"

"How do you know I have the gift?" I couldn't help being slightly bitter at her question about my mother. Did she not have a clue to what Cassie and I went through?

"We were kept in the dark about a lot of things," I said, with the intent to not hurt her, but I had to get the truth out. Besides, I wasn't here to familiarize myself with my family lineage or the gift they bestowed upon me. My gift, as Marion called it, was more of a curse than anything else. I was here to catch a killer. So that said, I wanted answers from her. Before I opened my mouth she spoke.

"The way you're looking at me, your mother said nothing to you or your sister. You know you have the sight. And what i mean, you see auras and ghosts. Tell me that I'm wrong." She sounded put out. But the way she took a dainty sip of her tea and had a smug smile appear on her face like she caught me in a lie contradicted what she said.

"You're not wrong," I admitted with some reluctance.

She then eyed my full plate and glanced back at me. "Eat." That one word had enough punch that I reached for a sandwich and took a bite. I guess I was hungry because I gobbled up the two sandwiches but took two more.

Once I finished finger sandwiches, a look of satisfaction appeared across her grinning face. I knew in that instant that whatever she was about to tell me next wasn't one and done. It was going to take a while.

"So what do you want to know about Cassie's murder," I asked, taking a sip of cooled tea. "And why did my parents keep us away from you? I get that my father would have, since he was a... jerk, but our mother?"

"Henry Bishop is a son-of-a-bitch. Yes, you can say it." She held up a hand. "Yes, he was. He was no good for my Barbara. Both Johnny and I saw that the second he came into Barbara's life and brought him around us. I knew it wasn't going to fare well for her. He was looking to score big with a rich girl with money. Do you know your father was from the next town over?" She waved her hand in a fleeting gesture. "Anyway, she wouldn't listen to her father or me. And after several attempts to stop her from seeing that bastard, your mother took off with him the day she turned eighteen. It was one of the saddest days of our lives. It tore a hole in your grandfather's heart. But that all changed when a few years later, she showed up on our doorstep with you. You were no more than a month old. Then we didn't see her again until your sister was born." Her eyes wet with tears and memories, Marion wiped them away and took a sip of her tea.

"Why did she wait so long?" A knot formed at the base of my throat at the emotions that came off Marion.

"I don't know. But you were about five, and your sister was a newborn when I found your mother back on my doorstep." The depth of Marion's sadness hummed through her and like link, that sadness coursed through me. "She had a black eye and sling across her left arm while she was carrying your sister. You were hanging on for dear life on your mamma's coattails."

"I don't remember that—at least—I don't think so." I tried to envision the day she was describing but drew a blank.

"Your grandfather was in such a rage. It took everything in me to stop him from going after Henry with a shotgun. Did you know, a few days later, he called the house knowing Barbara was here. He pleaded with her that he would never touch her again and that he promised to be the best father and husband." She snorted. "You know how long that lasted."

"You didn't believe him," I said, more of certainty than a question.

"Heck no, child. That rat-bastard hit her again and again. But my poor Barbara loved him too much and went back every time. The last time I saw her was when she came by with Cassie alone. She had to fifteen. I didn't know where you were, but your mother was bone-weary and needed rest. And your sister, she was still a tiny thing back then, but so happy. Nothing bothered her. Did you know she saw things too? A strong gift that girl had."

"Cassie saw auras too?" My suspicions were correct when Marion shook her head.

"No. Cassie saw other things. Like your mother did. Felt them strong. But you're like me. Colors are a way to a person's truth, their soul. A real lie detector. Am I right, or am I right?"

"You're right. But what of Cassie's murderer? Do you know who killed her? Did she show you?" I asked in rapid successions.

She shook her head. "The dream was so jumbled, I don't remember it all." She tapped her temples. "Yet, what I remember is all up here."

"Okay. But there's something I need to know now," I said with some trepidation. "If you knew about us, then why didn't you help us out when my father died?"

Before she got a chance to respond, a loud crash came from the back of the house. "What the heck?" Marion got up and looked out the sink window. The menacing barks out of Yeager Jr. sent chills down my spine. "It's probably the damn raccoons again or a bear getting into the garbage. I told that Kinney kid to make sure to tighten the garbage lids down and good, but what do you expect from a teenager. It's all about the instas-nappy or whatever social media these kids nowadays have their noses in. Don't worry. Junior, go get them!" Marion opened the back door, and out Junior went in a mad dash.

A long session of barking nipped the air, his yips softened, then silence. It had to be no more than five minutes before Marion opened the door and called for Junior, but the dog didn't return. She called again, which met with silence.

"Let me check." I pushed past Marion, who was protesting, but I ignored her and stepped outside. I went around the side yard and saw nothing. Not a bear, raccoon, or any animal in sight. I called out Yeager's name, but not a single bark or yip came back from the dog. I trailed the edge of the lawn where the woods butted up against the property. I didn't see or hear anything.

Crap. I hoped the dog didn't take off into the woods. Or if he did, I hoped the dog knew how to get back without sending out a search party.

I headed back to the house to inform Marion of the missing dog. I wasn't gone but ten minutes when I saw the back door ajar with the screen door wedged open with a piece of firewood. I was sure it came from the pile at the back of the house. I kicked it out, swung open the door, and peeled inside. "Marion?"

Something felt off. I could sense it in the air. That terrible feeling reached right down to my bones and yanked. I slowly walked to the kitchen table and found my grandmother slumped over onto her side in the chair. "Marion." I reached her side and kneeled before her. "Marion." I shook her gently, God-hoping she fell asleep, but the gnawing ache in my head was telling otherwise.

I righted her and tipped her face slightly with one hand. "Grandma." That endearment felt off in my mouth, but that was because I wasn't used to calling anyone that. I tilted Marion's head farther back to see her eyes when I saw blood dripping from the corner of her mouth. Her name tore from my throat as I frantically looked for a pulse by her neck. Faint, but there was still a pulse. Relief collided into panic as I raced to the phone that hugged the wall and dialed 911. If Marion is the only relative I have left, I would do everything in my power to save her even if I exposed myself to the truth of Cassie's murder.

9

MELINDA

N ot wanting to waste any time, I opened the garage door to my house and stowed my car inside it before anyone could see I was home.

I felt guilty for blowing Chase off. Albeit, the last place I wanted to be was in Marion Whitlow's home. I didn't know the woman well enough to trust her word on the talk she wanted to have with me. But our second to the last encounter wasn't at all courteous. So no. I wasn't going to put myself in that unsavory predicament. Whatever issues Marion had with my mother, I wanted nothing to do with it or Mrs. Whitlow.

It was for the best that I left because the last thing I wanted was to get in an argument with her in front of Chase.

I dropped my purse onto the counter and slid onto one of the stools I pulled out from under the kitchen island. I sat there, looking around the space, and had a sense of loss. How strange, but the last time I felt this way was when—

Don't think about the past, Melinda.

I shook myself clear of the fast-growing pity party for missing my family and focused on how quiet the house was, and I wished I did what Chase asked of me and followed him to his grandmother's home. At least I wouldn't be too much into my head.

"The list," I uttered to no one. Since I wasn't doing anything, and Chase was in Marion Whitlow's hands, I pulled out a pad of paper and a pen and started to jot down all the names of people that hated James Randal. It was the least I could do for Chase since I nearly ran him over with my car and had to deal with a woman like Marion.

The names came quick and easy, like sweeping the floor. Every granule of dirt I could think of and who it pertained to I wrote it down. I knew it wasn't going to take long to come up with a good list of people that hated Randle.

From Harold the mailman to even Sheriff Layton, who Randal pissed off in the middle of the Dark Hallow Diner a few months back. He then pissed off Luke Dawson, the said owner of the diner. Let's not forget the enormous face-to-face argument with the ski lodge manager, Willy Harrison, in the middle of the street, where they both nearly got ran over by old lady Harford. She needed her license revoked. Nice lady but terrible at seeing anything past her coke bottle think glasses.

Then Jasper Lindvall's face popped into my head, and I shivered with disgust. That day was so strange. Since the argument happened the day before Randal's so-called accident, I couldn't hear what they were arguing about, only getting a few discernible words here and there, like Foxwood Manor and gathering—whatever that meant—Yet, at the end of it, Jasper grabbed Randal by the necktie and punched him in the face. It led to

Randal flat on his back and Jasper stormed out of the realty office.

No one saw the confrontation except for me. I came through the back door, not wanting to give Randal a chance to flee. I had been there to give him a piece of my mind about the cards. Instead, I had stumbled upon them fighting. If Chase was right, and Randal's fall wasn't an accident, then for me, Jasper was the prime suspect.

After I finished my list, I made a fresh pot of coffee and wondered what Chase was doing right then. Then the thoughts of his eyes, mossy green, sent a wave of tingles across my skin. No man ever made me tingle by a single look. Sad to say, the prime pickings of men in this town were small and my dating life was at a nil. Maybe that was it. My attraction to Chase was because I was lonely. Then again, the man was insanely attractive—if you were into the broody bad boy—and I was definitely into Chase.

CHASE

"**N**ow, son, please explain to me again what happened?" Sheriff Layton asked as though he didn't believe a word I said the first time I explained. "I need clarity on how you came into Mrs. Whitlow's house if you had never met her before."

"I ain't your son." Frustration rolled off my shoulders like a rock slide. The cop didn't let me go with Marion in the ambulance when they arrived. Instead, he led me to the back of his squad all the while I was scared for Marion's life. I didn't even blink when Layton asked for my ID when we got the station. Not caring if he found out about me when my mind was on my sole family member fighting for her life.

Since I had no choice, I gave it to him. Layton led me to the small room and there I sat for thirty minutes before the sheriff walked in and started asking questions about what happened at Marion's house.

Crazy thing was, he mentioned nothing about Cassie's murder or my disappearance from Altoona, which gave me pause and some relief.

Which led to now. Brilliant blue, red and green swirled around Layton like an oncoming hurricane. He was angry, but he sat there cool as a cucumber, asking questions over and over again. The man was critical, breaking down my explanation of how I was associated with Marion Whitlow.

Although, it didn't help for my distrust for cops. That fear was branded on me since I was a kid by my father. However, I wasn't from this town. This man didn't know me or my situation, and vise versa.

Sitting in the police station, being interrogated while I didn't know if my grandmother was alive or dead was hitting my boiling point. "Just tell me if Marion's okay— that's all I want to know," I pushed in a near shout.

Layton stared at me like I had two heads. "You know, there are better ways to ask."

I wanted to pound my head against the table. Instead of my usual counter defensive, I closed my eyes and shut my mouth. I tapped down my anger and frustration and focused all that negative energy on why I was here in the first place. To find Cassie's killer.

If this absentminded sheriff needed to hear what happened again, then I'd tell him. I took a deep breath and recited the same thing I repeated not thirty minutes prior.

"So you're Mrs. Whitlow's grandson. It's funny she never mentioned you." I ignored his jab. Layton contin- ued. "You said she was in the kitchen when you went outside to investigate the noise?"

He sat there like we were old friends, leaning back in his chair with a cup of coffee in his hand, not a care in the world. His easy posture bothered the fuck out of me.

"Yes," I said as evenly as I could. "Marion and I were in the kitchen talking when a large crash came from the back of the house. I didn't know what caused the crash, but Marion thought it might have been an animal going at her garbage cans. So, she let out her dog, and when Yeager Jr. didn't come back when she called him back, I got up and went out to see what was going on. I couldn't find Yeager or what caused the noise, so I came back to the house and found the back door jarred open by a piece of wood."

"Didn't you find that odd? I'm mean the door being propped open by a piece of wood," he said in a deep southern drawl that anyone could tell he was born and bred in the South. "Now, why would someone do that?" He wrote something in his notebook before I was able to get a word out of my mouth.

"I don't know. I was going to ask Marion that, but I found her passed out—or attacked." I let out a grunt of aggravation because I was too damn tired and frustrated that I wasn't getting answers about Marion. "That's when I called the cops. Can you now tell me how my grandmother is doing?"

"Yes. Your grandmother. Now I've known Mrs. Whitlow for a long time. Did you know she is one of a few founding families left in Dark Hollow Lake? I would have known she had family left, but I don't. Now, why is that?" The hard glint in Layton's eyes sliced right through me like a sharpened knife.

A founding family? "Trust me. You're not the only one who is surprised. Not a few hours ago, I thought I had no family left. But Marion proved she is my grandmother on my mother's side," I admitted with a shrug. There was a slight ache forming at the center of my chest. I had to rub it to ease some of the pain away. Not sure if it was from lack of cooperation from this cop or my worry for a woman I hardly knew but laid claim to.

Layton stared at me for a long minute before he said, "She's still unconscious. The doctor doesn't know at this point when. There are no visible marks of an attack on her body. So the doctors are checking her blood, and check if she had a heart attack or a possible aneurism."

Relieved to know Marion was alive, I stood up since I wasn't under arrest. "Since I'm not under arrest, I'm leaving and going to the hospital." My words came out sharp as I headed to the door. But Layton stood, got into my path. There was a moment in everyone's lives that you had to choose which way to travel. I could easily fight the man in front of me, which I knew for sure would land my ass in jail. Or back down and plead with Layton that I was who I said I was. It was only a beat of two before Layton moved out of my way.

Layton came around the table and faced me. "Mr. Bishop, please don't leave my town. I'm not done with this or you. Got me? I might not have evidence against you, but time will tell what the truth is."

"Got it," I said with a single nod. I wanted to tell Layton to fuck off, but I knew he was only doing his job. The funny thing was, I thought he was going to bring up Cassie's murder at that moment. I still didn't understand why any of that information wasn't brought up when he investigated me. However, I wasn't going to help and bring her death up. Either John was handling the case so well that he kept Cassie's death under wraps until he found her killer.

"Now. Since I know you're Marion's grandson, I'm hospitable enough to give you a ride. Where are you staying at?" Layton's question jarred me out of my thoughts.

I blanked for a second. "What?"

"Where are you staying?" he repeated with a hint of annoyance back in his cadence.

"I want to go to the hospital. I need to see Marion," I insisted.

"I'm sorry, but the doctors are restricting any non-medical persons seeing her today. You can visit with her tomorrow."

I narrow my eyes at the man. I wanted to spit out that it was *he* who amended those orders. But what could I do? "Fine. I will go see her tomorrow," I gritted out.

"Then I'll ask again. Where are you staying at?"

I wanted to stay at Marion's, but I couldn't tell him that. Not sure if Marion wanted me there. So there was only one other place. "Melinda Bradley's."

His bushy brows rose high. "Melinda's? Oh, nice girl. How do you know her?" The questioning tone wasn't reassuring.

"We're... um, friends." It was all I'd give.

"All righty then." Without another word, I followed the sheriff out of the small building to his SUV. Several minutes later, I stood shoulder to shoulder with Layton while he knocked on Melinda's door.

When she opened the door, a weary look ran across her face when her gaze jumped from me to the cop. A deep crease set between her eyebrows, her eyes landed back on me before asking, "Sheriff, what can I do for you?"

CHASE

"Do you know this gentleman?" Layton asked his hand on the butt of his gun as casually as he could be. But he wasn't fooling anyone, least of all me.

Her eyes went to that gun, and a beat or two of contemplation filled her gaze before she spoke. "Yes. Why?"

"May we come in?" The severe note in Layton's voice had my spine stiffen. The man wasn't done.

Her lips thinned at the request, but she moved out of the doorway. "Sure. Come on in."

As I passed her, she mouthed, "What happened?" I shook my head slightly before we three converged in the living room. The smell of biscuits still lingered in the air.

A subtle rumble came from the sheriff's stomach. I wasn't sure if I should laugh or be even more annoyed by the way the man licked the corner of his lips.

Layton cleared his throat, thinking that was going to hide his hunger. "Did you know this is Mrs. Whitlow's grandson?" Jesus Christ, I knew he still didn't believe me.

"Yes," Melinda said with ease like she believed it to be true. "She told me earlier this morning when we saw her at the clinic. Why? What's going on?"

"Marion is in the hospital." I quickly said and then explained what happened, noting that Sheriff Layton looked pained—no, not pained—hungry, because his eyes kept shifting to the plate of biscuits on the kitchen island.

"How do you two know each other?" he asked, but his attention was now totally fixed on the round plate. "May I?"

Melinda and I looked at each other, surprise written in her pretty eyes. "Yes, help yourself."

Layton didn't hesitate. "I didn't get to have lunch today." He eyed me before shoving half a biscuit into his mouth. A groan escaped his lips as he wolfed down the other half of the biscuit.

I bit my tongue from laughing as Melinda and I stood there and watched Layton gobble up another biscuit.

"Sheriff, is there anything else?" Melinda asked a little briskly. The definite annoyance in her tone didn't go unnoticed. She wanted the cop-out of her house. I did too.

He raised a finger as he devoured the last of the biscuit in his hand. "No. But I told Mr. Bishop he couldn't leave town until Marion wakes and I get to the bottom of what happened." Then he waved Melinda over and took a few more steps away from me. "So since he's staying here with you, I want to make sure that if he leaves town, I want you to call me right away. Do you understand me?" He whispered to her as though I didn't hear a single word. I did.

"I heard you," I said with an equal amount of irritation shown on Melinda's face pinched expression.

"I thought you were going to stay at Marion's?" she asked me.

"Were you?" Layton turned to me.

It was a total lie, and I didn't understand why Melinda said that, but I went with it. "I was planning on it. But with Marion in the hospital, I wasn't sure if I should."

"Well, I think it's wise that you remain here with Melinda until Mrs. Whitlow wakes up. Don't you agree?" The edge to Layton's voice was firm. Neither Melinda nor I could object.

"Fine," she mumbled out, resignation apparent on her face.

"Good." With that, he grabbed one more biscuit and hustled out the front door, but not before he called back, "Great biscuits. Have to tell my wife about these. Have a nice day."

The second the front door closed, I swore, "This is fucked up."

Melinda grabbed my shoulder. "What happened to Marion?"

"I told you the truth. I found Marion unconscious with blood dripping from her mouth like she was smacked or punched or something. I don't know."

"Well, it doesn't matter. She's in good hands now. But, I'm stuck with you." She folded her arms across her chest and stared out toward the empty living room.

"I'm sorry I dragged you into my bullshit. I came here to look for a lead to my sister's murder, nearly got ran over, and now I have grandmother in the hospital with no fucking clue to what happened to her."

Melinda's eyes glazed over. "I told you I'm sorry

about the car, but you get half the blame. And, as much as I disliked your grandmother, I would never wish any ill will toward her." She blinked away the wateriness in her eyes and took a deep breath.

"I'm sorry for bringing up our accident. It wasn't your fault." She gave me a slight smile. She took a single step but quickly stopped.

I swore she wanted to say something, but instead, she bit at her lower lip and looked away. "It's okay." I tried to close the gap between us, but the look on her face warded me to stay in place.

Now that I was stuck here in Dark Hollow Lake for a little while longer, I had to focus on what I came here to do. "Did you get me the list of names?"

"That is what I was finishing up when you two showed up on my doorstep." She went around the island and pulled open one of the drawers. She took out a small notebook and flipped it to a page with at least twenty-some names. "There's many."

"I figured we could start with the easy ones, so I put those names on the top of the list."

"Randal pissed a lot of people off," I said, giving Melinda my total attention. "Thanks. This will be a good place to start."

Melinda's cheeks went from pale porcelain to flushed pink. I didn't know what it was about this woman, but I was coming to appreciate what she was doing for me.

The smile was back on her pretty face. Damn it. I'm seriously attracted to her. Just my luck too. But I wasn't going to start something with Melinda, especially when my life was a mess. Even though I couldn't help the way I was feeling for this woman. I had to clamp down on my sudden need to lean in and kiss her, and instead, I reached for a biscuit.

"When should we start?" she asked, offering me a sheepish grin I couldn't ignore.

"*I'll* start tomorrow. I don't want you in this—not after what happened to Marion. I'll go see Marion first and then start talking to these people." I took a bite and focused on the biscuit. "Damn. This is good."

"No, Chase. You need my help, and I'm not doing anything right now," she protested with her hands on her hips. "How are you going to get around with no car? And the people in this town aren't going to give up the gossip or problems to someone they don't know."

"No, you're not going to be a part of this, Melinda. Like I said, with what happened to Marion, who knows what's going on and who's involved. It's safer this way, and I'll call a taxi for rides."

"No taxi service here," she chuckles. "So too bad, Mr. Bishop. Or..." She snagged a biscuit off the plate and took a small bite.

"Or what?" I pushed, unsure if I wanted to know the next set of words out of her full lips.

"Or I'll call the sheriff and tell him everything."

My mouth dropped open. "You can't be serious. You're blackmailing me?"

"I am." She took another bite of the biscuit and eyed me like a cat that just ate a turkey.

"Well, shit."

12

CHASE

The day started the same as the morning before. I got up, washed, and met Melinda in the kitchen for breakfast. Though this morning, sitting across from her, I couldn't help looking at her in a different light.

Last night I came to a revelation. The attraction I had for her couldn't be tied down. And from the way she kept glancing at me, I think she liked me too. However, there was no way I wanted to start anything with Melinda, not with the shit that was going on. I wasn't even sure if the situation at Marion's house was a separate incident or in some way connected to Cassie's murder. Either way, I needed to make sure Melinda was going to stay safe.

"You know you don't have to do any of this for me. I appreciate you cooking but helping me find answers for my sister's murder might be dangerous. Especially now with what happened to Marion," I explained as I scooped a bite of scrambled eggs.

"If I don't, then who will?" One thinly shaped brow rose in question.

I smiled at her before taking another bite of breakfast. "I'm not going to talk you out of it, am I?"

She shook her head and turned back to her plate.

An overwhelming sense of relief filled my chest like a helium balloon. I could hardly take in a breath. Melinda didn't have a clue what her help meant to me. "You don't how much I appreciate your help."

"Stop. I'm sure if I were in your shoes, you would do the same for me." Was she right? Would I do the same for her? I thought about it for a second, and yeah, I would.

Her cheeks pinked up, and I couldn't help reaching out and touching her hand. I didn't need to add another set of thanks. She cleared her throat and pulled her hand back to her lap. "Now, what's on the agenda for this morning?"

"Let's work on the list before we go to the hospital."

Melinda grabbed the notebook and pulled out the list. "At the very top of the list is Sheriff Dan Layton," she said with a small frown. "I don't think the sheriff had anything to do with Randal's death or your sister's murder. He's a good man."

"Good man or not, what did the sheriff argue about?"

Melinda thought for a second and said, "Layton's son." She then quickly explained what happened.

I digested what Melinda said about Layton and Randal's argument outside the diner. "Randal was screaming at Layton about his son and how Joe and his friends broke into one of the empty houses on Bernard Street Randal was selling."

"When was this?"

She tapped her finger to her the tip of her nose, which I had to admit was cute. "Hmm. About a week before Randal's sudden demise."

"Are you sure about Sheriff Layton?" I ask, but with some doubt. After meeting the man, Layton didn't look like a cop that would do something so heinous as murder. Then my father's image intruded in my thoughts. Yeah. Layton was nothing like that asshole.

So I crossed Layton off the list. "Who's next?"

Melinda went down the names until we came to a Ruby Jane Nicolson. "She works at the consignment shop down on Main Street. She's a sweet thing and likes to make YouTube videos. She lives in the Old Sevier trailer park at the other end of town. I heard she had a run-in with Randal about rent."

"Sevier trailer park? Rent?"

"Yes. Some of the homes in the trailer park are owned by Randal," Melinda confessed, her voice went to a whisper like she was afraid the man in question could hear.

"Then this Ruby is worth talking to then. She might know something or have seen something. You know, I would like to see this Old Sevier Mines."

Melinda shivered. "I don't like the idea of going there. People say it's haunted."

With a waning smile, I said, "Don't be afraid. I'll scare them off." I wasn't sure if I could do just that. After the incident at the real estate office, I could only imagine what lurked in the mines.

"That is not funny," she said in a snort that came out more nervous. But a smile rose on her face, lighting up her beautiful azure eyes for the briefest of seconds before they dimmed. So did her aura. "Don't you know the history of Dark Hollow Lake, Chase?"

Wow. That was out of the left field. "No, but I have a feeling you're going tell me."

Melinda sat up, adjusting herself in the seat, and

began explaining. "Dark Hollow Lake was once in a different location. Before the Fort Patrick Henry Dam was put up back in the 1950s, residents of the town had to endure constant flooding. Once the dam was built, the people had to move, leaving behind everything they had worked hard for and settled here. But—and this is a big but, my granny told me and many others still whispered about how there's a legend that this town sits on an old Indian holy site. And that the town and the surrounding woods are haunted."

"Have you ever encountered something strange in the supernatural since you've grown up here?" I couldn't keep the chuckle back. We were here to break down the possible suspects. Instead, we're here talking about the town's history. It was good to release some of the tight restraints on the gloomy cloud around Melinda and me. Her frown suggested I was making fun. Maybe I was, just a little. "I'm serious," she said in a cute pout.

"Okay. Tell me."

She gave me a look I couldn't quite decipher before uttering, "When I sixteen, I got my first car. I wanted to show it off to my girlfriends. My parents let me, only if I go and come right back home since it was getting late in the day. I agreed. Of course, I took longer than I should and rushed to get back home. A block from my house, I saw a woman walking along the road. She didn't look well, sickly-looking like she should have been bedridden.

"It was getting dark, and my headlights shined on her, and I could fully see her face. Chase." Melinda put her hand to her heart like she remembered that day. Her breathing hitched as the fear creased along her forehead and her eyes began to water. "When the woman turned to me, she gave me a smile that I swear gave me the chills to this day remembering it. Yet, stupid young me, I stopped to ask if she needed help. Even though I was nervous, I pulled up next to her and rolled down the window, and then she was gone. Like she vanished out of thin air."

"You must have been freaked," I said, noting she was rubbing her hands vigorously. She was going to rub her skin raw. I took her hands into mine and held them gently. "What did you do?"

"I raced home and told my parents. They told me never to pull over for a stranger anymore and that for a girl my age, I could have seriously gotten hurt or worse. I understood what they were saying, but that still didn't justify how the woman just vanished right before me." Melinda paused, hitched out a breath before continuing. "I found out more than two days later about the incident. Apparently, a couple of people were fooling around the falls, and one of them fell. They couldn't find the woman's body until someone spotted her washed up near the mines."

"Now I have to see the place and the lake? First, let me call the hospital and find out about Marion," I said with some frustration.

"Good idea," she responded as she got up and started cleaning up the breakfast dishes.

To no surprise, the doctor explained that Marion was still in a coma and was under close observation.

"How is she?" Melinda asked as she wrapped the rest of the bacon in cling wrap.

"No change. Now let's go talk to Ruby," I admit with determination, needed to see justice for my baby sister.

"We should talk to her at the shop. It's closer and safer," Melinda suggested, not budging on seeing the mines.

I wanted to argue, yet, I relented. "Fine." I snagged the list off the counter while Melinda grabbed her purse. "But If Ruby isn't at the consignment shop today, we're heading to her trailer park and then the mines. Deal?"

"Whatever," Melinda grouched, but her still posture told me no way in hell she was doing that.

We'd see.

I t wasn't long before Melinda parked right outside the resale shop. Through the glass, I could see who I assumed was Ruby. A knitted bonnet covered the top of her head, with round-rimmed glasses covering her heart-shaped face.

"Let me do the talking, okay? She doesn't know you, and I'd hate for you to scare her away from any questions you want answers to," Melinda urged. Her eyes begged for me to concede.

"Alright. This is all you."

"Thank you," she said with relief.

"I hope she knows something. We have three more days left." Meaning, the card's date was fast approaching, and I wanted all the information to armor myself with.

"I hope so too."

We got out of the car, and Melinda took the lead as she strolled inside the business like we were here for a day of shopping.

"Ruby," Melinda called out, catching the girl off guard.

"Hi, Melinda." A blush bloomed in Ruby's cheeks when she immediately looked at me. So did her aura. Going from purplish-blue to bright pink. I had to smile at the attraction she gave off. She quickly dropped her eyes to whatever she was doing prior to our interruption. "What do you need?"

Melinda drew closer. The counter separated the space between them. She leaned in, her voice quiet so only Ruby could hear. "I need to talk to you about Randal."

Cold brown eyes met Melinda's. A corner of Ruby's upper lip tipped down in a deep frown. "What about?" The shift in her colors showed Ruby was wary.

"What did you have on Randal to let you remain in his trailer for free?" Well, that's news. Melinda didn't mention that part to me. "Come on, Ruby. Randal is dead. I found some notes on his desk while cleaning up. It mentioned your name--so fess up--and I promise, we will keep this between us."

I wasn't sure if Ruby believed Melinda. Still, a good minute passed before I was ready to give up.

Then Ruby said, "I overheard Randal talking to a guy about buying out the rest of the park and kicking everyone out so he could build condos. He said per verbatim, 'With the view of the lake, we will make a mint,'" she said in a rangy voice. "So I confronted Randal and told him if he wanted me to keep his secret, he'd let me stay in his crappy trailer for free. He agreed."

"That son-of-a—"

"Who's the other guy," I interrupted, impatience weighing in. "Where did you see them talking?"

Ruby hesitated a bit before she said, "I don't know who the man was, but I have seen him hanging out at the diner a few times. I also think he's staying at one of Randal's trailers. Lot 25."

"What does he look like?" Melinda asked as she took

a piece of paper out of her purse and jotted down the lot number.

"He has dirty grey hair like it's greasy and hadn't been washed in weeks. It's cut short like Sheriff Layton's, but the top is long. Old, maybe in his late fifties or early sixties, with a potbelly. He has an accent. Not from here. Maybe a northerner, a New York possibly —and he smokes." Ruby's eyes darted to me, then to Melinda, and then out the window like she expected someone was going to look in on us. "That's it." The finality of her dismissal had me turning away.

"Thanks," I offered and waited for Melinda as an image of what Ruby depicted transformed in my head. Nothing Ruby described was snapping my memory of anyone I knew.

"I promise, I won't say a word." Melinda pretended to lock her mouth with an invisible key and threw it away.

"Thanks," Ruby said and then turned back to her work.

There was nothing Ruby said that had any precedence over Cassie's murder. It left me with even more questions about Randal and what kind of man douche when he was alive.

"You know who Ruby described?" Melinda asked as she got in her car.

"Not a clue. An older man with greasy grey hair, with maybe a New York accent, has a potbelly and smokes. That doesn't ring any bells," I admitted regretfully.

"At least I wasn't going crazy. I knew Randal was up to no good. Too bad he's dead because I would love to strangle the hell out of him myself," Melinda hissed as she white-knuckled the steering wheel. "To think he was going to kick all those people out of their trailers to build condos. Now we have to go to that trailer," she said with resolution.

"I would like to visit Marion first. See her for myself." I said, guilt trickling in.

"Sure. Marion first." Apprehension in her eyes, she didn't want to go near those mines. "Then the trailer park."

"I promise we won't go near the mines if the place bothers you that much. Okay?"

Before Melinda could say anything, her cell phone rang.

"Hello."

"Melinda?" I could hear Sheriff Layton on the other end. She put the phone on speaker so that I could listen to it. "Is Chase Bishop with you?"

"I'm here," I said in a rush, not liking the tone in the man's voice.

"I just got to the hospital to check Marion... I'm sorry, son, your grandmother, passed a few minutes ago."

13

CHASE

The drive to County General next town over was quiet. Melinda barely spoke a word to me since the news of my grandmother's death hit me like a Mack truck.

Melinda's muted colors were choking me, so I kept my eyes focused out the window and let my brain take in what I was about to face.

I tried not to wallow in my feelings for the grandmother I recently reconnected with, but fuck it, it hurts. Bad. The pain echoed off my chest with every pounding beat of my heart.

The only sobering fact that she told me she loved my sister and me our whole lives made it easier to breathe. But here I was alone, again. I guess time didn't matter since I was mourning for a woman I didn't get a chance to know, hurting just as much as losing Cassie.

"Chase, are you going to be okay?" Melinda's eyes glistened with unshed tears. Should I be shedding them too? For some reason, I couldn't. Not now. Maybe not ever.

I was never able to cry, not the way Cassie had. Maybe it was the fact that my father beat into my brain that men didn't cry. "Crying is for babies and losers. Are you a loser, Chase?" Henry's words had left more permanent bruises than his fist. If he had known how I felt for him, my beating would have been so much worse.

I sucked in an unsteady breath. "I guess I have to be.

With each step closer to Sheriff Layton, standing just inside the hospital sliding doors, dread-filled the rest of the vast gaping space that was split open from Cassie's death. Swirling tendrils of blues and red surrounded the cop. I was cautious about taking those steps into the hospital. Who knew ten days since I took off for answers for Cassie's death that I'd be standing here with another death of a relative on my hands. I was face to face with the law, but for a grandmother, I never knew.

"Chase. Melinda. Come with me," Layton advised with a pinched expression.

As he asked, we followed him to a bank of elevators, then down a floor to the basement. It had to be the morgue. A gnawing ache in the pit of my stomach started to rise, but I ignored it and kept focused on the numbers on the elevator buttons.

Sure enough, when the door slid open, I saw a sign up ahead that read, morgue. Hospital Personal Only.

Layton turned to me, his eyes reflected profound sadness and genuine sympathy. I wasn't sure if I should be angry for his altruistic attitude. Yet, with every glance of his sorrowful look, my stomach wanted to revolt.

I swore I was marked to have a lonely life of misery —first my mother, then father—which he never counted. Henry dying was the best thing that ever happened to Cassie and me. Then Cassie and now

Marion. I had nobody left. That revelation cut deeper, right down to the marrow of my soul that I might never recover.

Not wanting to stand there in the abysmal quiet, I needed this moment over with so I could do what I came here to do and then get back on with my life—no matter how lonely it would be.

"I'm guessing Chase had to come here to confirm Marion's body?" Melinda asked, thankful that she spoke up.

"No. I confirmed it with the coroner that it was Marion who passed," Layton said somberly. "However, there is another reason why I told you to come. Chase, I need you to look at Marion's for a whole different reason."

His comment caught me off guard. "Why?"

"Because I don't think your grandmother died of a heart attack or any natural causes. But before I say more, I need you to look at her."

"O-okay." With each step, my feet were like giant size boulders. It took everything in me to move them. The idea that someone might have hurt Marion while I was outside looking for her dog was unbelievable. I wasn't gone that long.

Through one door, we met a man who I assumed was the coroner.

"Chase, this is coroner, Dr. Klein."

"Follow me," the doctor said as he led us through another set of doors.

We entered a room where along one wall were nine square metal doors that housed the bodies. Klein walked over to one, paused to look at me for a second as though I needed that space of time. There was no amount of time to group my emotions for what I was about to see, but I appreciated that he did that. I gave him a nod, and then he opened it slowly.

I held my breath as he slid out Marion's covered body.

Layton walked over and uncovered her face and neck. "Chase, please tell me what you see?"

With Melinda by my side, her arm immediately wrapped around mine for support. I took those few steps and stared down at what Layton was talking about. More under her jawline around Marion's neck was a purply red bruised line like someone took a thin rope and choked Marion with it. Besides the blood at the corner of her mouth, there was a mark that was all too familiar.

I jumped back, stumbling out of Melinda's arm, shocked at the sight. "That can't be." I shook my head.

"Chase, tell me. What is it?" Layton insisted, but his eyes were staring down at my fingers. "You don't wear rings." That statement had me drawing back further until my back hit the door we came through.

"What are you talking about?" Melinda asked with fear radiating from her eyes. "I don't understand."

"But Chase does. You know who killed your grandmother." Layton's words were hard and potent like a copperhead's bite.

It had been a long time that fear took control over me. My mouth went instantly dry, and every warning bell inside was blaring to run. Runaway and never look back.

"Chase." Layton's words cut through my panic as he reached me, his rough hands on my stiff shoulders. "Look at me, boy." I automatically did as he demanded. "Who killed your grandmother?"

With my eyes locked onto his hazel ones, my hand slowly went up, pushing back the small amount of bangs that covered a scar I had gotten when I was fourteen. I swallowed the grit from my throat and found my voice. "It's the same person who gave me this."

Layton leaned in closer and saw his eyes went wide in understanding. "Who gave you that scar." His voice was a quiet threat, but it wasn't toward me.

"My father. But…"

"But what?" Layton growled eyes glinted with daggers.

"Henry Bishop died ten years ago."

14

MELINDA

"This doesn't make any sense," I uttered as we drove back to Dark Hollow Lake, where Layton wanted more of Chase's statement.

"It doesn't. But the fact that my grandmother has the same ring mark as I do says otherwise. That ring was commissioned by my mother right after they were married. It was his wedding ring."

"Could someone have taken your father's ring after he died?" I tried to think of every scenario that popped into my head.

"Possibly. All I know is that when my father died in that fire, the heat from the blaze charred his remains that the only thing left was ashes and few bone fragments. The coroners weren't able to truly identify him." Chase's voice shook as he continued. "That man had terrorized my sister and me as far back as I could remember. He never wanted kids, but my mother…" A small, sad smile formed on his handsome face. "She always wanted them. Us. Too bad she didn't know she would die and leave us to that monster." The brunt of his words had me tearing up. I grew up being cherished and loved as good parents should show for their kids. But Chase knew different, and my heart hurt for the man.

I wanted to reach out and comfort him, but the way his stiff body wedged to the door had me rethinking it.

"Chase?"

"Yeah?" Chase didn't look at me. He kept his attention out the window.

"How about after we're done at the police station, we go get some pizza and get shit-faced." I mustered up as much of a smile I could when he tilted his head back to me. His lips tipped up slightly, not much, but enough that he was on board with my idea.

"I like that plan very much."

It took longer than I thought. Not only did Layton go over the time Marion was attacked, but he also went over the fire Chase's father had died in. I sat in the waiting area for nearly three more hours before the sheriff let Chase go.

With a parting understanding between Layton and Chase, we left.

We went to the store and stocked up on beer and two bottles of my favorite wine. Once we got a few extra munchies, we headed back to my house.

"How about you take a shower while I call for the pizza," I said, placing the bags on the counter.

"Thanks for the offer of pizza and getting shit-faced, but I need some time alone." Chase cupped my face, and I could see he wanted to say something else. Instead, he dropped his hand and headed to the room he slept in.

"Take your time. I'm still ordering pizza and grabbing a glass of wine," I called out, hoping Chase would take up my offer and not hide from me. However, I knew

—out of anyone, Chase needed time to grieve. He needed the space, so I didn't push.

I stood there and watched him disappear into the room. I wondered how much alcohol would it take to help me sleep without dreaming of that sad beautiful face of Chase Bishop and stop mourning for my family that I would never get back.

CHASE

Not sure how long I sat there in bed contemplating my miserable life while my brain droned over on what happened in the past two weeks. I wished I had just stayed home and watched over Cassie. Then I wouldn't be here, chasing something—or someone who caused this terrible mess in my life.

I mulled over what Melinda said about my father's ring, and maybe someone might have stolen it after his death. That was a possibility, but I couldn't imagine who. There were no diamonds in the setting, and the design was odd. The crown was the shape of a ram's head. The scar on my forehead and what was on Marion's face was identical. It wasn't coincidental.

My gut was telling me there was a connection, but what was it?

How ironic. What if Henry's ring was in the hands of another, the same person who killed my grandmother, and if I followed my gut, then that same person murdered Cassie.

None of these puzzles fit together or made any sense. Yet, like a puzzle, a few missing pieces were missing to tie them all together. Once I found those missing pieces, I would know who was behind all this horrific shit.

Then a thought hit me. I needed to call John. I immediately picked up my phone and dialed his number. It rang four times before it went to voice mail.

"Hey. It's me. I haven't heard from you. How is it going with Cassie's case? Are there leads? I'm still here in Dark Hollow Lake. Met my grandmother I never knew… damn I'm rambling. Call me. I need to talk to you about my father's—" The voice mail cut me off. I hung up, wanting to pull my hair out from not knowing what John was doing with Cassie's case.

I turned onto my side, frustration coursing through me. The second I closed my eyes, a delicious smell bombarded my nostrils. "Pizza," I groaned. And so did my stomach. A soft lilting melody floated along with a tempting aroma.

Sick of overthinking, I got up and took what Melinda was offering. Food and alcohol. What could a person want amid the chaos?

I stepped out of the bedroom and headed into the kitchen, where Melinda had her back to me. She was bouncing on the balls of her feet in tune with the country music she had on the radio. In a pair of black shorts and a pink mid-waisted top, Melinda's hair was up in a bun on top of her head.

"Do you have room for one more?" I asked, startling her.

She whirled around, part of a piece of pizza stuck out her mouth and a glass of wine in her hand. "Oh my God. You scared the crap out of me," she said as she put down the slice and clasped her free hand to her heart. Her eyes strayed to my bare chest. I forgot to put on a shirt. I contemplated for a second if I should put one on but liked how she was looking at me. Like I was next on the menu. Her cheeks bloomed crimson, and she quickly turned away. "Yes. There's plenty."

I made my way to the island, grabbed a paper plate, and checked out the selection Melinda ordered. A small pizza with all veggies. One large with all meat and another small pizza with onions, green peppers, and mushrooms.

"Are you planning on feeding an army? Who's coming over?" I asked in a chuckle as I grabbed a couple of pieces of all meat.

"Beer?" she asked as she headed over to the refrigerator.

"Sure." I accepted the bottle, twisted the top, and took a good long pull. It had been a while since I touched any alcohol, but the cold brew tasted good going down.

"Feeling better?" she asked with a smile.

"Yes. Thanks," I admitted with another bite of pizza. "Now, why all the pizza?"

She blushed even more. "I didn't know what you'd like, so I ordered what I thought you'd eat. Besides, there will be leftovers, and I don't have to cook tomorrow."

"Good thinking."

"Thanks," she chirped and picked up her slice.

"I should be the one to say thank you."

"It's all right. Now eat," Melinda ordered mildly.

For the rest of the night, I pushed away any of my problems and just enjoyed the food, drinks, and company. I wasn't sure how or when, but I found myself laying on my side on the couch, my head cocked to one side—with Melinda curled up in front of me. The glare from the weather channel on the flat-screen woke me up. The TV was turned down, so I couldn't hear anything.

I glanced through blurred-eyed over to the ancient VCR player, which read 1:00 am. The light over the stove was left on, but the radio in the kitchen was off. Melinda must have turned it off.

I was about to wake Melinda when I saw the little boy standing by the laundry room out of the corner of my eye. I froze, my heart beating out of my chest from the shock of seeing him standing there like a grey statue. I wanted to blame my half-drunken state. I chalked it up that my foggy brain conjured up the boy, and he was just an illusion. But not now.

He then put a finger to his lips, telling me to stay quiet. His attention shifted to Melinda, smiled, and then vanished where he stood. Right there in plain sight, he was gone.

Melinda tucked so nicely next to me, I didn't want to move for fear of jolting her awake.

It took about three-second before I decided to wake Melinda and tell her about the boy when a noise from the laundry room halted my movements. The door was closed, which made the sounds muffled. I knew there was a door that led to the side yard, which could easily be compromised.

I listened. Again, sounds of scratching caught my ears. She had no dogs or any other pets.

As quietly as possible, I shook Melinda, covering her mouth with my hand. She woke with a start, bloodshot eyes wide mixed with alcohol and a bit of panic. Her hand went to mine that covered her mouth, but I tightened up and signaled for her to listen. She did.

Her eyes widened even more with fear as she shook

her head, letting me know she wasn't sure what that sound was. I released her mouth and put a finger to my mouth, signaling her to stay quiet.

Quietly, I got up and stretched my head out of its kink before investigating what that sound was. I took one step, and the light from the kitchen and the television blinked out, leaving only a small battery-operated night light on the counter to blink on. A little gasp from Melinda had my feet freeze on the spot and listen for more sounds. Nothing. Just the sound of Melinda standing up from the sofa.

Remembering that I left my cell on the kitchen island, I grabbed my phone and made my way back to Melinda. "Call the cops." My mouth was right to her ear.

Melinda grabbed my arm and frantically pointed in the direction of a baseball bat leaning against the door molding. I immediately hustled over and grabbed the bat, then tucked myself against the wall and listened. Just as I was ready for whoever it was inside the laundry room, Melinda's voice carried over to me.

She was on the phone with the Sheriff. One second of quiet filled the space, then a chink of breaking glass had me exorcising my legs to move. The intruder must have heard her too because the next thing I heard was the door slammed against the wall and then crashing glass. With the bat raised, I wrenched the door open and found the backdoor wide open, and the inlaid glass shattered all over the floor.

"Don't go further. You have no shoes on." Melinda's hand tightened around my bicep, halting my pursuit. "Whoever it was is gone now... Yes, he's right here... Okay." She hung up. "Sheriff Layton said he's sending a squad and to stay out of the laundry room."

"Fuck," I hissed with agitation. Whoever tried to sneak in here didn't realize we were up.

I was about to take a small step, still wanting to chase, but Melinda pulled me away from the door and yanked the bat out of my hand. "Sit. I'll make some coffee. I have a feeling it's going to be a long night."

16

CHASE

"I don't know, Chase, if you just have crappy luck, or this break-in is coincidental," Layton said with a shake of his head. "Melinda, I suggest first thing in the morning to get someone here to replace that door with no glass and a better lock."

"I'll be on it like ham on toast," she uttered as her attention was to the floor.

Without thought, I chuckled. "Another one of your mother's sayings?"

Her eyes looked distant as though she was else-where. "What? Yes... What's so funny?" Melinda huffed her hands on her hips. With a small growl, she said, "If we're done here, I need to clean up the glass."

"You go on. I would like a word with Chase alone," Layton said as he waved me over to the other side of the kitchen. I had a feeling what he was about to say wasn't good and wanted out of earshot for Melinda's sake.

"Of course you do." Melinda waved in frustration and walked out of the kitchen. Layton watched her leave before turning his attention to me. Worry stamped across his face.

"I'll make sure she's safe, Sheriff," I said earnestly.

"I don't think it's wise for you to stay here anymore. I have a feeling whoever it was that tried to come in was looking for you. It's a gut thing."

I couldn't deny his forthwith speculation. "I have to agree with you. But what if whoever might think I'm still here? Melinda will be alone without any protection. Besides, where would I stay?"

"I have a feeling whoever this person is, is watching you closely. So why not stay at your grandmother's. You did say she welcomed you. I don't think Marion would mind." His drawl was thick, but the swirl of his colors spoke the truth.

"I'll consider it," I said with resignation. Who was I kidding? I wanted to stay there, even if it was for only a few nights. With all the stuff Marion had, maybe there was a chance I could get to know my grandparents through pictures and whatever else I found inside. "You're right. I'll go first thing in the morning."

"Good." He turned to leave but quickly shifted back. "One more thing I forgot to tell you. Marion's lawyer, Mr. Kent Duncan, called me today. He wants to talk to you. Here's his number. Call him when you get a chance."

"What does he want?" I stared down at the number, apprehension crawled up my spine.

"Something about Marion's will—I don't know. He didn't tell me." With that, Layton left.

Just one more person I had to deal with. Putting the piece of paper on the counter, I'd worry about it tomorrow. I helped Melinda clean up the rest of the glass and made sure the plywood I found in the garage was secure around the doorway.

Melinda remained quiet throughout the clean-up and headed to bed without a word to me. I got it. She was freaked. So was I, but I didn't push her to talk. I said my good night and went to bed.

As I started to drift off to sleep, I heard a soft knock at the bedroom door.

"Come in," I utter as I sat up.

Melinda opened the door, her face shown with tears by the moonlight seeping through the thin veil of curtains. "I can't sleep."

From her tear-streaked face and wide worried look across her eyes, Melinda was afraid. I couldn't help but feel guilty because it was my fault she was in this mess in the first place.

I pulled back the blankets and made room on the queen-size mattress. "Come here."

She closed the door and climbed in, face to face, but kept a few inches apart from me. "Thank you," she whispered.

It was all she said before our eyes met, and something clicked. I wasn't sure what it was that drew me closer to her, but the next thing I knew, I closed the small gap between us and kissed her. It wasn't easy or soft. It was all-consuming and was in heaven.

I needed her just as desperately as she needed me. My lips were demanding, and she didn't deny me.

Melinda suddenly pulled away, but for only a second to rid her clothes and the realization that she was mine for the night. A trickle of guilt played in my mind, and I disconnected our mouths to asked her, "Are you sure?" That one question, simple and to the point, had put me on the edge of need while I waited for her answer. Thank Christ, I didn't have to wait long because being denied by Melinda would have killed me.

She stared into my eyes for a moment before she leaned forward and kissed me solemnly. Melinda pushed me back onto the bed, my back to the mattress as she slid on top. Her unanswered yes was enough.

Our lips collided once more as our bodies melded together in harmony. My hands claimed Melinda's body as her mouth took possession of my mouth and tongue.

I wrapped my arms around her middle and pulled Melinda tighter to me. I let her lead before my urge to take control took over.

Still, in my arms, I rolled her over, putting Melinda on her back. I hovered over her, our bodies inches from touching like a tease. Staring into her lust-induced eyes, I smiled down at Melinda with wonder. "You are so beautiful." I breathed in softly and absorb the warmth of her scent into my lungs.

Her smile went wide, and there was a note of mischief across her face. "Is that a sappy love song?" I couldn't help but laugh because she was right. At that moment, just the two of us, everything was perfect. Melinda made it all perfect, especially when I didn't feel like I deserved any of it.

Before my desire for Melinda had me combusting, I kissed her with all that I had. Her body went pliable to mine as her fingers trailed along my torso like she was mapping out every inch. Between our hands and mouths, we feasted on each other. I took what I wanted, and she gave it freely, and I did the same for her.

"Make me forget," Melinda uttered against my mouth.

"I will, baby." I took her lips, hungry for her taste,

while my hands worked to remove my boxers. The second it was off, she opened for me.

The heat between us was scorching, burning me to the core. With each touch and taste of this woman, every particle of my being told me this was right. She was perfect for me.

Melinda's aura started off orangey but was engulfed in fiery red, nearly blinding me when my fingers began to play with the core of her. Wet and slick for me as I plunged one finger, then two.

With every breathy moan, Melinda uttered, "Chase, I want a…"

"What do you want?" I asked, my fingers moving in and out of her channel, wishing it was my cock giving her the pleasure.

"I need you," she hummed as she grazed her nails down my back. That spurred me to move and retrieve the condom from my wallet and be balls deep inside her.

Without hesitation, I rolled on the latex and held my dick at her entrance; my eyes met Melinda, wanting further approval from her. Melinda knew what I was asking because she slowly nodded and licked her lips as though she was ravenous. I did as she bid and sunk slowly inside her until we were as one.

A loud groan escaped my lips as her tight channel enveloped my dick in velvet heat.

I stilled for only a few beats before I started to move. Melinda moved in the rhythm with me, and it was glorious. What was even better was when she wrapped her legs around my waist and met me with each firm stroke.

"Oh God, Chase," she moaned. "I'm gonna…"

Melinda started to tighten around me. Her body quivered with every intense thrust. It bolstered me to faster until I felt that family tingle at the base of my spine and balls. A few more strokes, and I was a goner. "Melinda," I called out as I spilled into the condom, and we both careened over the edge.

We laid there in silence until both our breathing calmed. With reluctance, I left the bed and got rid of the condoms but quickly got back into bed and pulled Melinda back into my arms.

In the end, we both fell asleep sated and too exhausted to ponder what happened and what tomorrow would bring.

17

CHASE

I woke up, Melinda's leg hung over mine, her arm draped around my neck, her fingers in the hairs at my nape and our faces inches away. On cue, our eyes met through hazy sleep. Her sweet smile lightened my sleep-rattled brain, remembering what we did last night. Or rather, early this morning. Many times. Yes, I was insatiable. And from my memory, so was she.

It took only a second before Melinda realized her body was plastered to mine. She quickly peeled herself back and fumbled out of bed. "I... um... bathroom." Cheeks bloomed crimson; Melinda rushed out of the room without another word.

I blew out a breath, a slight chuckle slipped out. But I covered my mouth so Melinda wouldn't hear me. The last thing I wanted was to hurt her feelings.

I stretched out, feeling a generously amount of peace. Yet, I didn't know why. When I walked out of Melinda's door today, I'd still have all the problems I had yesterday—more so with the break-in last night.

Glancing over at the door Melinda exited out of, I

realized my feelings for that woman were growing fast. It was more than friendship, or I wouldn't have pursued what we shared last night. Once Cassie's killer was brought to justice, my life wasn't going to be the same. What was I going to do? Where would I go? All my life, it was about Cassie and her well-being. Always thinking of Cassie first. Now, I wasn't sure what my purpose in life was. Where would I go from there?

"Are you hungry?" Melinda asked in the doorway, pulling me from my ruminations. Before I got a chance to reply, her question was answered with an obnoxious growl of my stomach. "That'll be a yes." She smiled, but the joy I was used to seeing across her face wasn't there. She strode away from me with purpose. Did she regret what we did last night?

"Melinda," I called out, but I was met with quiet. I wanted to tell her thanks, but that didn't sound right. Then my phone pinged with a text message. "Shit." I grabbed my cell and looked down at the screen.

One missed call too. *John.* Tapping the phone, I glanced down at his text.

"Stay where you are. It's not good here. You're not safe."

What the hell did that mean? I wasn't safe? Fuck that. I wasn't going to text back. Instead, I called. Three rings in, John picked up.

"Vaughn." The same tight reassuring voice I expected from the man answered, but the reassurance was gone.

"What do you mean I'm not safe?" The hell with the pretenses, I needed answers. I had a lot to say.

"Hold on." I could hear muffled voices and then a sound of a door closing. He must be at the precinct. "What did I tell you about calling me?"

"What do you mean I'm not safe?" I wasn't going to let it go. It was time for some answers. He had been quiet way too long and not answering my previous questions. With what had happened in the past two days, I needed something from him.

John's exhaled breath was telling. He only sounded like that if he was tired. I was sure he must have been exhausted running around tracking down leads.

John took a beat or two before he said, "I have a feeling who killed your sister."

My back snapped straight. I couldn't lay in bed any longer. I climbed out from the sheet and pressed the phone tighter to my ear, and asked, "Who?"

"Remember right before your father died?"

"How could I not? That neurotic asshole scared Cassie so much she ended staying with me. Cassie didn't want to be around him from that point on."

"There was a reason. Weeks before the fire, we were investigating a double homicide where two smaller drug cartels were involved. A war of some sort between them. I have a feeling one or both might have been involved."

What he was saying didn't make sense. "What did that have to do with Cassie's murder?"

"Your father and I, along with several DEA agents, busted up a major drug trafficking ring, leaving behind several dead bodies, 3 million in blow and heroine, and twelve million in cash. It was one of the largest busts for us."

"You think one of those people who were involved killed Cassie? Why? She was young when that happened." My brain was buzzing with the news he was giving me.

"She might have seen something she wasn't supposed to. One more thing."

"What?" Not sure if I wanted to hear more. I shook my head vehemently like John could see me. "No. Like I said, she was young then. I don't buy it. I don't get how your bust has anything to do with Cassie or her death."

"That twelve million in cash disappeared the following day. Nobody knew how it disappeared out of the evidence room. So, I think whoever was behind Cassie's murder also killed your father for that money," he said in a growl. "I'm not asking—I'm demanding you to stay put in Dark Hollow Lake until this is all over, Chase."

The empty ache in the middle of my chest blossomed in pain at his admission about my father's death. "Do you think Henry was murdered?"

"Yes. I lost your father and your sister. I'm not going to lose you too. At least stay there until I get more answers."

I swallowed down the pressure building in my chest. "Why didn't my father never told me about my grandmother. I met Marion Whitlow. She was family." Silence filled the space. "John?"

"Was? What happened?" he choked out.

"Are you okay?"

"I'm okay. Drank some coffee and went down the wrong way. Now tell me. Did something happened to Marion?"

"Someone killed her, John. The coroner said it was strangulation. But you know what was odd? Someone punched her face and left behind a mark similar to the one my father gave me on my forehead. Strange, isn't it?" There was more silence. I continued. "Do you think the men that killed my father came here and killed her too?" It sounded so preposterous even saying it out loud. Then remembering my father's ring and putting what

John said together gave me a clear perspective of this situation. "John, are you there?"

"Yeah." He cleared his throat. "Chase, I have to go. We'll talk later. Keep safe." He then hung up. I had a bad feeling John wasn't telling me everything. Our conversation left me even more confused and slightly angry. All of this shit that followed the man's death was Henry Bishop's fault.

I wish I remembered more about a drug bust back then. Tracing back any of my memories before my father had died was nearly impossible. However, I remember that time when I had to watch Cassie for a few days because our father was raging about something and tore the house apart. That was right before he died in the fire.

If what John said was the truth, and the missing money was connected to my father's murder, which was inadvertently connected to Cassie, then, in turn, would be connected to... me. *Holy hell.* It was me that brought the killer here to Dark Hollow Lake, and it was my fault that Marion died.

Melinda. I was so fucking stupid. Here I was playing house with her, and this whole time I was leading her into trouble—possibly death. I needed to get out of here and stay away from her. Far away from her. Then a revelation hit me as I replayed John's words over in my head. If that money vanished, and John didn't know where it was, nor did the DEA, then there was only one person that could have taken it. "Henry." But he was dead, and those answers were lost forever.

18

MELINDA

I was an idiot. I shouldn't have slept with Chase. We barely knew each other. Yet, I was making breakfast like a happy housewife. Wishful thinking, Melinda?

No. Chase Bishop was far from steady I needed in my life. Granted, when I went to his room, it was because I was afraid to be alone. Who wouldn't after a break-in? Now, Chase would probably assume I'd do him anytime he wished, which I wouldn't... sort of.

He was cute and all... Okay, I was lying. Chase was gorgeous. With his hazel eyes and thick dark blond hair, he was any woman's wet dream. And last night. I couldn't help but groan out from the memories of our time in bed. He was so... good. And his hands... A shiver raced across my skin at the memory plastered in my brain.

With everything going on in both our lives, mostly his, the last thing either of us wanted was to shake the tremulous limb of my new friendship—if that was what you'd call it.

I finished scrambling the eggs and grabbed my

parents' phone book, and searched for Caleb. The handyman's number my parents used called for repairs. Once Caleb agreed to fix the back door, I hung up and went to tell Chase the food was ready.

I knocked on the door frame and walked in. "Breakfast?"

Chase's back was to me, but he didn't look at me as he put his clothes on. "Sounds good." The strain in his voice told me something was going on.

"What's wrong?" I croaked out.

He sat down on the end of the bed, eyes cast down to the carpeted floor. "I like you, Melinda but last night—"

"I get it." I interrupted him, waving him off as though his words weren't a knife that scored every inch of my insides. I knew this could happen. I shook my head. "You don't have to explain," I utter quietly. "I guess I got carried away last night. I'm sorry."

"Don't be. It was the best night I've had in a long time. It's just that I'm thinking for your safety. I don't want what happened last night to interfere with the main reason why I'm here. And I think Layton was right. I'm going to stay at Marion's."

I felt gut-punched at his admission. Even though I understood what he was saying, something inside didn't want to let him go. Instead of following my instincts and argue with the man, I spoke with an extended hand, "I get it. Friends?"

He took my hand with a brilliant but tentative smile that showed off some dimples I hadn't noticed before. But the shine didn't reach his eyes. "Most definitely friends. Now. And speaking of friends. I can't be wearing the same clothes three days in a row. Can you drive me to where we umm... met so I can find my duffle? Hopefully, it's still lying on the side of the road."

"Yes, friend. I'll be happy to," I said evenly. "But the food is ready. You can't leave on an empty stomach," I attempted a cheerful attitude, but it came out forced.

"Thanks. Hey, I got some news from my friend," he said as he followed me to the kitchen.

"Good news, I hope."

"He might have some possible leads for my sister's murder, which I have a feeling it'll reach all the way to here."

I bit my lip at his statement. "What do you mean reached here?"

"Marion's murder might be tied to my sister and my father's death, which stems down to a whole lot of money missing from a drug bust ten years ago."

"Please, explain like I'm an idiot while I make some coffee."

"Melinda, you're not an idiot," he scolded, then further explained. The more he explained, the more I was resolute to consider a handgun for protection and stow it somewhere in the house.

"So you think your father had stolen the money. But someone found out, and they killed him for it?"

"Yes. I think whoever tried to get the information from Cassie, but she didn't know anything, and they killed her for it," he said with grief pasted on his face.

"But how is your grandmother a part of all this? And, if you said this happened ten years ago, your sister was young at the time and had ASD, right?"

"I agree. Jesus, this whole situation is crazy, if you seriously think about it. Hell, I don't know what to think now." Chase dropped down into the chair and put his hands over his face. "All I wanted was a good life for my sister and me, and now, I have nothing. I'm sorry that you're caught up in my bullshit," he said in a ragged whisper.

I went over and drew him in for a hug. Friends hug. "You're not alone in this, Chase. I'm your friend. You got me until this is all over. Besides, I haven't had this many thrills since Randal fell down the stairs and broke his neck." I tried to fuse some humor, but Chase wasn't laughing. I released him and looked into his eyes, wanting him to see how sincere I was.

I fused my mouth to his lips because I couldn't help but kiss him. Gentle at the start, but the second I felt his tongue wanting entrance into my mouth, I gave into my sudden need to have him naked over me.

As we hit the couch, Chase's phone rang. Our lips disengaged, like two connecting magnets. For a good minute, well, maybe it was less, but we stared at each other, contemplating if he should get the phone or continue our path of destroying our friendship.

Chase pulled away first, snagged his phone from the back pocket of his jeans. "Hello."

I was close enough to hear the person on the other line.

"May I speak to Chase Bishop?" the man on the line asked.

"Speaking."

"My name is Kent Duncan. I'm Marion Whitlow's lawyer. Do you have some time today to come by the office and see me? I have some pressing matters with Marion's estate to discuss with you."

"Yes, sure," Chase said, but his eyes remained on me. I felt guilty listening in, but the look on his face expressed he didn't mind.

"Would you be able to come to my office around eleven today?"

"Today at eleven?" Chase asked, his face held some surprise.

I frantically nodded at him to agree.

"Sure. Eleven sounds good."

Mr. Duncan then rattled off his address and said his farewell before hanging up.

"Forget breakfast. We'll stop at the Sweet Shop and head over to the office. Greysburg is only about a twenty-minute ride."

"That's not happening," Chase said matter-of-factly. "I don't want you involved."

"I don't care. Besides, you don't have a car." Then a thought hit me. "If you and the sheriff are worried about my safety, maybe he's right, and you need to move into your grandmother's house."

"Okay," he said, an eyebrow quirked up. "Why do I hear a but."

"Well, since my house has been broken into and it's not safe here, and you're moving into Marion's until this whole situation is solved, then I'm moving in with you. So after we pick up your bag, go to the lawyer's, I'll pack my stuff and head to Marion's with you. And you're not talking me out of it, Mr. Bishop. I'm in this with you all the way."

19

CHASE

S tubborn, stubborn woman. Melinda's face was one of seriousness as she strategically explained how my living arrangement was going to change.

"I don't think it's a wise idea, Melinda. Besides, I'm not even sure legally I can stay in Marion's house," I said, rubbing my face in frustration.

"First things first, we go see your grandmother's lawyer," she said with a bit of mischievous glint in her eyes. I shook my head at her, but she cut off my refusal. "It's nine, and I'm in the mood for some pastries. Kinsley's bakery is open. Have a little sweet and coffee, then we'll go see the lawyer. Sounds good?"

Reluctantly, I agreed. What choice did I have? With no vehicle of my own, I needed Melinda to ride into Greysburg.

The sweet shop was located right in the heart of town. The moment I step out of the car, I could smell a delicious aroma coming out of the bakery. Maybe Melinda had something, suggesting coming here.

When we walked in, there were several people in

line. It took a bit, but we finally made it up to the counter to order.

"Melinda, so nice to see you. Who's your friend?" A blonde woman said. She might have been an inch shorter than Melinda's five-eight, way on the thinner side, and smiled eagerly at us. Yet, her smile didn't belie the muted storm of colors around her. This woman was exhausted, but one wouldn't see it on her jovial face.

"Kinsley Austin, this is Chase Bishop. Chase, this is Kinsley. She owns this fine establishment," Melinda explained while she studied the fresh pastries behind the glass. "I'll have an apple cinnamon crawler with a large coffee, cream, and two sugars, please."

"And you?" Kinsley asked me with eagerness.

My eyes went to the case, where all sorts of sweets were there to choose from. Then my eyes landed on a long john donut with a strip of caramelized bacon on top. The small sign in front of the delectable yeasty goodness was described. "I'll take that one with a large coffee, black. Please."

"And manners too," she said with a wink. "Be right back."

As she turned away and started bagging our orders, Melinda chimed with, "Kinsley, how are you doing now that Randal is no longer the pain?"

The woman whipped around, eyes pinpointed at Melinda with a frown that could melt the sun. Her muted colors burst into bright angry tones. "I'm happy to say my days are a whole lot better since that plague of this town is gone." She placed our orders on the counter and immediately excused herself.

I glanced to Melinda, who had a remorseful look on her face. She leaned in, rasping out in a whisper, "She was on the list."

"She is?" I tried to remember who was on Randal's list of enemies, but I vaguely remembered anyone's name.

After we got our treats and coffees, we took a seat by the window. With a bite of her crawler, Melinda said, "I'm sorry, but Kinsley usually keeps her emotions close to the belt, if you know what I mean. I wanted to see how she really felt about Randal's death."

"What's her story with Randal?"

"He owns—well used to own the property the bakery sits on. Now Kinsley got a chance to buy full out," she explained with another bite of the donut. "Mmm. Kinley's the best at what she does. People from surrounding towns come for her baked goods."

"I can see why," I added, with a bite of my long john. The mixture of sweet breadiness of the donut and salt from the bacon was the best that I nearly moaned with every taste of the delectable treat.

"Chase, I know this might be a little late asking, but what do you do for a living back home?" Melinda asked as she quickly swallowed another bite of her crawler. Her question caught me off guard. She continued. "I mean, we've been together for going on three or so days, and I don't know anything about you. And I would like to, I mean, get to know you."

I put down my donut and took a sip of the coffee. "I was a truck driver for a small company in Altoona."

"What did you haul?" she asked with another bite and moaned. She was actually turning me on with her noises. I concentrated on my own food or at least looked out the window before my pants tented with the apparent hard-on for this woman.

"All kinds of things. I hardly look at the inventory I'm loading. Yet, one time, I did haul a ton of blue corn."

Before Melinda was able to counter, Kinsley drew up short at our table, her light blue eyes still blazed with anger. "I don't appreciate you coming into my place and starting trouble."

"I-I'm sorry, Kinsley. I didn't mean to stir anything up."

"I don't need anyone coming in here and remind me the shit I had gone through with that asshole."

Melinda looked at me, her eyes wide in shock, but there was a note of approval she needed from me to say something. I took a second to think, then nodded. She turned back to the bakery owner. "If you have a second, I'll tell you what's going on, but you need to keep it close."

Kinsley stared at me for a second, a quizzical expression on her face. "Fine. But only a minute. She grabbed an empty chair from the table next to us and sat. "Now spill."

Melinda told her most of it, except for Cassie's death, which I appreciated. After retelling the past two days, Kinsley promised to keep her eyes and ears open for anything odd said about Randal.

We stayed for a few more minutes before we headed out. Instead of looking for my duffle, we went straight to Mr. Duncan's office since it was nearing eleven. I figured we would look for it on our way back.

Twenty minutes later and five minutes past the hour, we pulled up to the two-story brick building. To my surprise, three police officers stood outside the law office while yellow caution tape blocked part of the entrance. I had an ill feeling, which went from bad to worse when a stretcher came out with a body covered on it.

20

CHASE

"Holy crap. Chase, you don't think…"

"I don't know what to think, but that doesn't look good," I admitted. The awful gnawing in my gut grew at the thought of Marion's lawyer was murdered.

"If that's Duncan, then there's a definite connection, or you terrible luck struck again." Melinda chewed on her lip as we tracked how many cops milled about outside the building.

I would have to agree with her statement. It was just too coincidental that another person died that was connected to my grandmother.

Melinda decided to park a block down. We slowly made our way back toward the barricaded building, where a bigger crowd formed at the outer barrier. Just out of reach, I wondered how long the cops were going to be stationed outside the place before I got a chance to find out if that was Marion's lawyer that was hauled out of the office building.

A hitch in Melinda had me turning to her. "What wrong?"

"I'm... sorry. This... it's just seeing all the... I'm caught me off guard." She covered her face so as not to show her tears.

"Melinda, sweetheart," I said, pulling her into my arms and held her tight.

"I'm sorry. But all this reminds me of the night my parents and brother had died." She tried to turn away, but I held her close until she calmed down.

"Look at me, please." I coaxed her chin up, her eyes filled with tears. "I should be the one to say sorry. I shouldn't have gotten you involved in my crap."

"Why are you sorry? You didn't drive drunk and kill my family," she muffled out from my chest. "I know I should move on, but the pain won't go away. It's been two years—But I miss them so much."

"There's no expiration when the pain should go away. I think everyone has their own time frame and you," I pulled her face from my chest and looked into her liquid blue eyes. "You have all the time in the world to mourn. But my mother once told me that don't let life pass you by."

"Wise words." She wiped the tears away with both hands and straightened, pulling back from my hold. "Thank you." Melinda blew out a breath and released a small smile. "Now the tear fest is over, you came here to talk to Marion's lawyer. Let me find out from that cop what's going on."

Before I could ask Melinda what she was talking about, she strode away from where we were standing to a lone black cop that stood sentinel by a wooden horse barrier.

Melinda approached the cop like she was supposed to be there. She was talking animatedly, using her watery eyes to her advantage. The officer, whose stoic face slowly morphed into one of remorse, began nodding like he understood what she was saying. I'd give my left nut to hear what Melinda was saying to the cop.

I didn't have to wait long. The officer moved the horse out of the way so Melinda could pass. He led her inside the building.

Not five minutes later, Melinda came bustling out of the building, with the same cop right behind her. She turned, said something to him with a smile, and a wave goodbye. He returned it with a generous one of his own. He went back the wooden horse once more and stood there like he had never moved.

I began to walk so as not to look too suspicious. The instant I turned the corner onto the next block, Melinda reached my side. "What the hell were you thinking going in there?—I can't fathom what you said to that cop to let you in."

Melinda looked around and made sure no one was around us. She then pulled out a file folder from under her jacket. "It's only good southern respect, Mr. Bishop. This is why I went in instead of you." She poked me in the chest.

I stared down at the brown folder in her hands, my eyes fixed to the name stickered at the top. *Marion Whitlow.* "But how?"

She pulled out her inhaler and waved it in my face. "I told the cop that I came by yesterday about the loss of my family, and in all of my fretting, I forgot my lucky inhaler. I told him I needed it before I had another attack. The cop believed me."

"And he just let you in the office?" Skepticism grating my voice.

"Well, no." She rolled her eyes at me. "He was

looking around the office floor with me. That was when I saw the file right on top of Duncan's desk. So I shoved it in my jacket—thank goodness my jacket is big enough."

"You southern girls are crazy. You know that? What you just did was illegal. What if you got caught?" I wanted to shake some sense into her, but at the same time, kiss the crap out of her.

"How? I was looking for my inhaler?" She patted my chest. "Let's go."

"I must be crazy." But I followed Melinda to her car. "What about Duncan? Did the cop say who died?"

Melinda worried, her bottom lip with her teeth. "Yes, it was Duncan. I guess he died in one of the back rooms. The cop didn't offer up anything else."

"Well, crap. What am I going to do now?" I rubbed the back of my neck in agitation.

"You should talk to Layton and maybe another lawyer on this matter." Melinda offered up some advice I wasn't sure that was good. The problem was, I had no idea what was in Marion's will, but from the look of the folder, it was extensive.

We headed back to Dark Hollow Lake, on the same road my truck conked out on me. I didn't see the old thing, but I was suddenly reminded where Melinda nearly ran me over. "Need to find my bag," I said, staring out the window.

"That is why I took this way. Do you remember where exactly?" Melinda asked sadly. The melancholy mood shifted immediately.

"What's wrong?"

Her eyes slightly watered as she glanced at me, then out the windshield. Melinda needed a moment and I gave it to her. "This is where my family had lost their lives from a drunk driver two years ago." She blinked and let the tears fall.

As I reached out to touch her shoulder, a flash of something caught my peripheral. The second I turned, I swore I saw the boy. "Stop," I shouted.

Melinda slammed on the breaks, stopping immediately. I got out and quickly looked around. It wasn't quite noon, but the sun was bright enough that it should have burned the mist that covered the field in front of me. I glanced down at the ground, and to the left of me, I spotted my backpack.

Melinda got out of the car and moved to my side. "You found your bag. Weird. I thought we were much further down the road."

"I thought so too," I confessed as my eyes trailed along the tree line about fifty feet away.

Melinda's attention was fixed on the same place. "These woods always give me the creeps." She shivered as her eyes scanned the copse of trees to the left.

I didn't know what it was, but I turned to Melinda and confessed, "I saw a little boy the night you hit me with your car and the same boy at your house the night of the break-in."

"I grazed you with my car, but what do you mean you saw a boy? Here and in my house?" Fear started to trickle in her wide eyes.

"I think he's a ghost." The moment I said it, I knew it was the wrong thing to say.

Melinda's eyes went wider than saucers, and her mouth dropped open in shock. "What do you mean he's a ghost? Like dead?" She took a step back and started to fanatically look around. "Are you talking ghosts? There was a ghost in my house? Are you joking with me?

Because it isn't funny, Mr. Bishop." There she goes calling me Mr. Bishop.

I nodded. "I'm totally serious."

"You think so?" The frantic edge in her voice and the way she spun around, her eyes scanning the area we were standing. Melinda was about to freak out.

She did.

"You're not joking, are you?"

"There's more," I added with reluctance. If I was going to tell Melinda everything, it might as well be everything.

"Of course there is. What? There is more than one ghost?" She let out a huff of laughter, but it was far from funny.

"Yes. And, I can see… auras."

She stood there, speechless. Her mouth opened and closed Like a gaping fish out of the water several times before coming to, "What's my aura right now?"

I wasn't expecting her to ask, but I told her. "There's a lot of blue, with some yellow and red mixed in."

"What does that mean?" She narrowed her eyes at me as her arms wrapped around her middle.

"You're mad and don't believe me." I had to tell her the truth.

"It's bad enough we looking for a murderer, while people were dying around us, but now you're saying there's a boy ghost my house? And you see auras? Well, that's just fucking great." She let out a surprised gasp and pointed to me. "Chase Bishop, you made me swear."

"Melinda."

"Oh no. Don't you Melinda me. Why didn't you tell me sooner," she whined. "I don't like ghosts."

"What would you have done?"

"Called Pastor Johnson."

"And what would he do, pray the ghost away?"

"Don't patronize me, Chase. I can't believe you didn't tell me. I'm already spooked with that break-in, and now I'm worried about a ghost—heck with that. Now I'm more certain that we are moving into your grandmother's house today. And I don't care what you say, Mr. Bishop. Do you hear me?"

Something in me wanted to reach out and kiss the anger off her face. Instead, I said, "Yes, ma'am."

21

CHASE

As Melinda pulled up to Marion's house, I rummaged in my jacket pocket for the house car key from yesterday. I was stupidly grateful to have forgotten it in my pocket since who knew how long I was staying in Dark Hollow Lake. And while I was staying in Marion's home, I hoped to find out more about my family I never knew I had.

"I'll be back in an hour. Just need to get a few essentials. Call me if you need anything?"

"Will do—unless you want me to go with you," I insisted as I got out and grabbed my duffle from the back seat.

"Not necessary. Just keep your cell phone on," Melinda said as she points to my hand.

"Don't take too long." I spied her through the passenger side window.

She rolled her eyes before waving me off. "I'll do my best." So damn cheeky.

I made my way to the house, knowing the front door would be nearly impossible to fit through with all the boxes and stuff Marion had stacked up in the entranceway.

Facing the back door, I took out my phone and fired off a text to Sheriff Layton that I would stay at Marion's.

Layton: Good. And we got to talk. Got some bad news.

I had a feeling he was going to tell me that Kent Duncan had died, which I already knew. I had to tell the man the truth.

Me: Already know. Went to Duncan's office this morning and saw the cops.

Layton: I still need to talk to you. See you in 15.

If it wasn't about the lawyer, then what other lousy news did he have for me? Before I pondered anymore, I unlocked the door and went in.

After dropping my duffle on the kitchen table, I locked the back door and did a quick look around to make sure no one was in the house. Once I did my quick inspection, I made my way back to the kitchen and began cleaning it up. Even though Marion wasn't here, I had a feeling the woman didn't like a messy kitchen. I didn't understand her reasoning for keeping this room clean when the rest of the house was a hoarder's paradise.

As I dumped the dried-up sandwiches and stale cookies into the garbage, I loaded up the dishwasher that had seen better days.

After I finished with the kitchen, I grabbed my duffle and went into the living room. Granted, it wasn't as crowded with boxes as it was in the foyer. Nonetheless, I still needed to be extra careful, or I'd knock down stacks of car magazines, more boxes, and piles of books with my bag.

I glanced over to one of the low stacks of boxes,

tempted to see what was inside. I reached for a top box, but my guilt made me stop midway. These aren't mine.

A knock at the front door had me pausing. Instead of opening the door, I called out, "Who is it."

"Sheriff Layton."

"Come through the back door. Marion has all these boxes piled up, and I'm afraid one stack gets hit, and a domino effect will happen."

"Good idea," he said before making his way around the back of the house.

Meeting him at the door, Layton came in, his attention assessing the room. "It's clean in here."

"I cleaned it... I figured the cops were done with retrieving evidence and from the way the kitchen before she died, Marion liked it clean inside here," I admitted, heat spreading across my face from embarrassment. "Come have a seat. Wants some coffee?"

"No thanks. Official business and all," Layton stated as he sat down at the kitchen table and took off his hat.

"Good. I don't know where Marion hid the coffee grounds. But I'm sure it's hidden in one of the cabinets."

"Chase, I got some sad news and bad news."

"I'm assuming you here because of Mr. Duncan's death," I said with no surprise to my tone as I took the opposite seat from Layton.

"Yes. Greysburg PD is calling his death a homicide." That news took me by surprise. Layton continued. "Sorriest thing is that whoever killed Keven Duncan thought they killed Kent. I'm also here to tell you that one of my deputies found Marion's dog. It was shot dead."

"What?" To hear that Marion's dog was dead hit me just as hard as Marion's death left another hole in my heart for the animal. I wasn't an animal lover, but I would have loved Yeager Jr., "I figured since he didn't come back to the house. As for Mr. Duncan..."

"I guess you didn't know about that too. Keven and Kent Duncan were identical twins. From the report, Keven came in early to do some work and was killed in his office. I'm guessing the killer found Keven and strangled him... just like Marion. But you know what strange to me is that the killer laid out paperwork—like a ledger of clients Keven was supposedly blackmailing. The problem with that is that all the people on that list are dead."

"Maybe the blackmailee got tired of the blackmail and killed the right lawyer? I don't know what this has to do with me other than the killer used the same method of killing."

Layton shook his head. "Now, do you know what's even more peculiar?"

"I can't imagine." I kept my eyes on the man, but I got a sinking suspicion he was about to mention Melinda and her stupidity of stealing that file.

"One of the officers reported a woman—right about Melinda Bradley's description, came by and explained that she left her inhaler in Kent's office and that she medically needed it or she'd die. Do you know any such woman?"

There must have been a look on my face because Layton's lips pursed tight, but his eyes lit with amusement.

"Melinda." It was all I could say.

"I figured right," Layton said, rubbing the nape of his neck.

What was I doing? Melinda was in this mess because of me. If I wanted Melinda safe and out of jail, I needed to be honest with Layton and explain everything. This might be a long shot, but I had to try.

"There's more you don't know." I kept my eyes on the man, who looked at me with the mere understanding that I was about to divulge my reasons why I was in Dark Hollow Lake.

He leaned back in the chair, folded his arms across his beefy chest. "I think I'll have that coffee now."

"You got it. Just give me a sec to find the machine." I rushed around the kitchen, tracking down the coffee grounds, and set up the coffee maker. Once the cups were in hand, I began to explain what had started this treacherous journey.

From Cassie's murder to John's insistence on leaving Altoona, and then Melinda's bogus card to her almost running over as I headed to Dark Hollow Lake. Yet, I did exclude the part of seeing ghosts and auras around people. Not everyone would accept the truth about the supernatural. Besides those details, Layton didn't need to be privy to. With Melinda's fake card still in my wallet, I took it out and showed him. Layton studied the details on the back with a stern assessment.

All in all, Layton sat there, quiet, and took in everything I said. With silence came a raw ache of nerves strung taut, waiting on the man as I watched his face ponder.

"The card was the only reason you came here? That's a big leap." The incongruity in his voice had me stalling my thoughts as though he didn't believe me. That was it?

"I went with my gut and followed the lead," I validated, biting out with a bit more vinegar than I intended. "I'm sorry, but this was my sister's life someone took. I'll be damned if I don't do anything."

"And you thought this John told you—"

"John's a cop. I trusted him. He's been in my life for as long as I could remember. When he told me to run, so I ran."

I thought Layton would jump up, cuff me, and read me my Miranda rights for Cassie's murder right then. Or maybe arrested me for my sheer stupidity as he looked at me with such blatant eyes. Instead, Layton took out his phone, tapped at the screen, and then hit speaker. I wanted to ask who he was calling, but he raised a finger to silence me before a word was out of my mouth.

"Hey, Chief Rogers."

"Well, son-of-a-gun, it's Sheriff Layton. You're alive and well," said the man huffing out on the other line.

"Yeah, yeah, it's been a long time, no hear and all that," he said in an easy-going gate, but there was a slice of annoyance in his tone too.

"Long time? Man, I haven't heard from you in over a year. Don't you got anything to say to your older brother?" My eyes went wide at the man's admission. I stared at Layton, his skin tinged pink at my evident unspoken surprise.

"I know—and we'll talk. But," Layton gruffly drawled. "But now, I need some info on a girl. One Cassie Bishop from Altoona, Pennsylvania. Twenty-five. Possible homicide."

"Sure, hold on a sec." I could hear rustling around on the other line. Layton idly looked at me as he waited while there was rustling with papers or something.

"I don't have a Cassie Bishop."

"Are you sure? Check again, under Cassandra Bishop, brother Chase Bishop." His eyes shifted to me while his fingers were toying the edge of the plastic dinner mats. The mention of my name made my spine snap straight, and my heart started thrashing against my ribcage.

Fucking perfect. All I need is for Roger to say I'm on the most wanted list for Cassie's murder.

"O-kay. Hold on," Roger uttered, tapping like he was typing on a keyboard.

The few extremely long seconds of silence had raised my anxiety to DEFCON 5. I didn't understand how Cassie's case didn't come up. I saw her body—the blood she lost first hand. What had John been doing all this time?

"The only connection that comes up with a Cassandra Bishop is Chase Bishop, which has a missing alert," Roger reported. "Age thirty. Six-one, a hundred and eighty pounds. Blonde, hazel eyes. Last seen two weeks ago in Altoona. I'll fax you a copy."

My eyes went wide in shock at the information. I was about to question that allegation when Layton put his fingers to his lips again to shut me down.

"That's all you got for Chase Bishop, but nothing on Cassie?" Layton pushed.

"Sorry. It's all I got," Rogers offered. "How about this. I'll do some digging around and call some of the contacts in Altoona to find out more... but on one condition."

"What's that?" Layton growled out. Though the smile negated the anger in his voice.

"You'll meet me for lunch next week, and I'll call you back tomorrow with details." The chuckle on the other end of the line ceased. His brother hung up.

Layton shook his head as he put his cell back into his pocket.

"You two were close?" I asked as worry wormed into my heart. I thought I was close with Cassie, but I was only her caretaker if I had to really think about it. Nothing more. Even though Cassie was never a big talker, she conveyed so much in her own way that I never fully understood what she needed.

"As close as two half-brothers can get." Layton became tight-lipped like he wanted to say more, but he turned his attention back to the topic on hand. "My brother is chief of police in Johnstown, Pennsylvania. He'll get what I need."

"I was close to my sister." I didn't realize that came out of my mouth.

"Son, I have a nose when someone is lying or telling the truth. And right now, my nose is telling me you're telling the truth. So relax. Alright?" He stood, adjusting his belt. "I suggest you stick around here but call Kent Duncan and tell Melinda to call me right soon."

"I will," I said, meeting the sheriff in the eye.

"Now, I have to call Greysburg PD and make sure Melinda doesn't go to jail for sneaking into a crime scene." Layton rolled his eyes before heading out the back door.

I sat back down, my mind awhirl with what I heard from Layton's brother. Through the Altoona PD, I was reported missing. But there wasn't anything on Cassie. "What in the hell are you up to, John?"

Not wanting to ponder on what was going on, I pulled out my phone and called John. The second I hit send, I got an automated voice telling me that the number I dialed was no longer in service. I tried again, and again it went straight to the message telling me the phone number is no longer. I dropped the cell onto the table and sat there numb. John, the only person I had trusted for all these years, blindsided me. Now, I wasn't sure what to do next.

22

MELINDA

It took a little longer to get my things and go to the grocery store. I wasn't sure what Marion had in the house, but I couldn't chance it. I texted Chase, telling him I was heading his way. He texted back to go to the back door to get in. It was a strange request, but I did what he asked.

As I rounded the back of the house, I saw Chase through the window, slumped in a chair at the kitchen table. The dejected look on his face had my heart stop. I strode fast across the lawn until I was kneeling by Chase's side.

"What wrong?" I asked, drawing his hand into mine. "You found out something?"

"Sheriff Layton came by."

Holy crap. I knew it. I was in trouble. "And?"

"He knew it was you that went into the lawyer's office," he said evenly. "He also told me that it wasn't Kent Duncan that died, but his twin brother, Keven."

"Really?" I grew up, my heart in my throat. "What now? Am I going to jail—is that why he was here looking for me—God, Chase, I can't go to jail. I wouldn't last—"

"Stop. You're not going to jail." He pulled me in and had me onto his lap with his arms wrapped around me. "He came by to tell me about Keven Duncan. Layton said that he was killed the same way as Marion, and he'd fix it, so you don't get into trouble."

"So he thinks it's the same killer," I said, expelling a breath with no relief from the ache in my chest.

"Layton didn't say it outright, but I think so," Chase said with a single slight nod.

"Did he mention the file I took?" I asked as another shiver of worry ran down my spine.

"No, but I'm sure he'll find out soon enough. Although, he said he'll take care of the situation. But Melinda..." he paused, rubbing his face. I looked down at his handsome face and couldn't help but run my hand along his stubbled jaw. His thick lashes wet with tears. Why was Chase crying?

"What happened, Chase?"

"I told Layton everything."

That news had my mouth drop open in shock. "What do you mean everything?"

"Everything. From Cassie's murder to now," he uttered with pinched eyes that focused on the linoleum floor.

"How did he take the news about your sister's murder?"

"Layton believes I'm innocent. He made a call to his brother, who's the chief of police in Johnstown, Pennsylvania. He didn't find Cassie's name but found my name, which showed up on the missing persons' file. It doesn't make any sense, so I called my friend John, and his phone number is no longer in service."

"What do you mean no longer?"

"I mean, his cell number is no longer active. Like the man I've known all my fucking life is ghosting me." Chase nudged me off his land. He started pacing. I stood there, not sure what to do.

"I'm sorry this is happening to you, Chase." I meant every word.

Chase grabbed the cups on the table and headed off to the sink. "I don't know what to do next. I came here to find a killer or find a lead that will point to the asshole that killed my sister. But here I am, stuck playing housemaid in my dead grandmother's house, that I didn't even know existed until now. How fucked up is that?"

He dropped his head, not able to see his face. Chase's hands white-knuckled the edge of the sink. I knew if I didn't do something, he was going to do something he may regret.

"How about this? We are here for now, so why not get to know your family better."

He popped his head up, red-eyed and glassy, one corner of his lips tipped up slightly. He gave the nod. "Why not. But first, let me call Kent Duncan."

"While you do that, I'll make something to eat, and then we can settle in the living room and start going through the file and then some things around here," I said, my eyes aimed out toward the hallway where I saw tall rows of shoe boxes. "Especially those." I pointed to them, curiosity piqued.

"Sure." Chase wiped his hands on a rose embroidered towel and pulled his phone and a card out of his pocket. He went into the other room for privacy.

I nabbed the grocery bags from where I dropped them and put the food away. With a quick decision on a meal of pasta and veggies, I began to cook.

Catching muffled words here and there, I strained to listen in on Chase's murmured conversation with the lawyer. Thus, I couldn't make out anything and turned my focus on the food.

It wasn't long before he walked back into the kitchen with an odd look on his face.

"What is it?" I asked as I kept chopping the red peppers and tossing them into the hot frying pan.

"Apparently, I am the sole benefactor of Marion Whitlow's estate and that he'll be comin' by next week with the proper paperwork," he said in befuddlement. "He would have come today but with his brother dying and all. Melinda, the lawyer didn't sound all that sad."

"Well, that's... weird."

"You're telling me. I still don't get it." Chase walked over and stood next to me.

"Get what?" I asked, turning away from the pan, and couldn't help but lean against him. "Maybe he wasn't close to his brother."

The heat of his body enticed me to wrap my arms around the man and give into what I knew he needed, but the look in his eyes had me staying put and center my attention on the food.

"No. I'm mean Marion. If she knew about us, why didn't she reach out to us? Why not help us when we needed her the most when my mother passed away?" He shook his head in frustration.

"Well, we can't think on empty stomachs. Give me ten minutes to get this meal together while you check out what's in those boxes. I'm dying to know," I urged, nudging Chase with my hip.

"It's probably pictures and stuff," said Chase as he headed into the hallway. He plucked a box from one of the taller piles and brought it to the kitchen table. "Let's see what she has in here."

The moment the lid was off, both mine and Chase's eyes bugged out of our heads like those Saturday morning cartoon characters I used to watch as a kid.

"Am I seeing what you're seeing?" I asked, turning to Chase for an answer.

"Yeah. Money."

23

CHASE

M oney was the last thing I expected to see in the shoebox—a boat-load of money.

Melinda turned off the stovetop and moved by her side. We looked at each other, and with a silent understanding, we each took a few more boxes off of different piles and brought them to the table.

Each box we uncovered had a neat stack of cash tightly inside it. There were hundred dollar bills in some and the fifties in others, but all filled with money. They were all filled boxes in dense rows.

"Where do you think Marion got all this money from?" Melinda asked as she took out a thick set of bills from the box in front of her. "If each of those boxes out there has the same amount of cash as we have here, there's got to be thousands—maybe hundreds of thousands."

"I'm not sure about that. But if this money has anything to do with Marion's death, then we need to call Layton and tell him what we found." I began to pull out of my phone, but Melinda snagged it from my hand.

"Wait. I don't want to sound like I have the finders-keeper-losers-weepers attitude, but with this much money, where did Marion get it from? And maybe you're right. If this money is connected to her death, then I wouldn't know who to trust," she said with all seriousness. "Layton's a nice guy, but with everything that has happened so far, I wouldn't tell anyone until we get to the bottom of it all."

She was right. Aside from Melinda, I didn't know who was on my side. Certainly not John. Layton took my confession in stride, but who's to say he wasn't contacting the Altoona PD for further investigation into Cassie's murder on my behalf.

Then a thought occurred to me. What if John was behind Cassie's murder? That idea sent a white-hot chill across my body, and I suddenly became nauseous.

"Chase, you look like you just saw a ghost."

I looked at Melinda, afraid to say what I was thinking. What if? Worry radiated from her pretty blue gaze. I was correct to assume John had been behind it all this time, and he was the one who killed my father. If one component in each of the situations in my life, John was linked to it. Hell, he was even there when my mother—I quickly shook my head. I was overthinking this.

"You're scaring me, Chase." Melinda's grip on my arm tightened. "Tell me."

I swallowed hard, trying to get past the sudden dryness in my mouth. "What if it was John who was behind it all?"

"Your friend?" Her voice hitched with astonishment at my sudden epiphany. "You mean the cop back home?"

"What if it was John who killed Cassie and made it look like it was someone else."

"What would be his motive?"

I shook my head. "I don't know."

"Do you think he could be linked to Marion and Keven Duncan's murders too?"

"I don't know that either. But I think I have to go back home." The vehemence in my rising voice had Melinda shaking her head no.

Before Melinda got a word out, the doorbell rang. We looked at each other for the answer to who was at the door.

"I didn't tell anyone I was coming here," Melinda mouthed her confessed as she quickly shoved the money back into the boxes and stashed them in the first cabinet that stored all the pots and pans.

"The only people who know I'm here is Layton," I admitted in a whisper as I got up and carefully made my way to the front door. I wish the damn door had a peephole.

Melinda was right behind me. "Look through the front window."

I shook my head but called out, "Who is it."

There was a beat or two of nothing before the person finally answered. "It's me. John."

24

CHASE

My heart leaped out of my chest as his words ran through me like a bucket of ice water. I stood there frozen, wasn't sure what to do when I felt Melinda's hand on my back. The warmth pulled me out of my stupor, but it gave me no comfort.

She mouthed, *"Are you going to answer?"* The spike of red, orange, and green splashed across my vision as her worries became apparent.

I wasn't sure if I should now. Between my confusion on why John was here and the anger steadily inclining, I was split in two with my decision. However, with the newly discovered money in the boxes and the revelation that John could be Cassie's killer, it had me seriously considering either opening the door to deck the man or not answer the door.

Melinda took charge, nudging me out of the way. She latched the chain on the door, then unlocked and opened the door a crack. "Can I help you?"

For only knowing Melinda barely a week, I could easily see the strength this woman possessed. Even though her bright personality shines through in her facial expressions right now, her aura was shouting out fear. Although, her straight stature and demeanor posed on her face showed a different attitude.

"Oh. I thought this was Marion Whitlow's home," John questioned with some suspicion.

"It is. What can I help you with?" Melinda tightened the grip on the door, her tone curt.

"I'm detective John Vaughn, from Altoona, Pennsylvania." Without looking, I knew he took out his badge. John had said it gave the person some comfort when they were talking to a cop. "I heard a male's voice when I knocked."

"It's only me. What do you want, Detective? You're a long ways from Altoona?"

"Your name?" John asked like he was there in a professional capacity.

"If you looking for Marion Whitlow, then I suggest you contact Dark Hollow Lake PD. Ask for Sheriff Layton. He'd be the one to tell you details of Mrs. Whitlow. In the meantime, I have work to do." *Bravo.*

Melinda was about to close the door when John put a stop to it with his point boot. He let out a frustrated sigh. "That's not necessary. I was just told that a Chase Bishop, my nephew, is staying here. Can you please get him? It's an urgent matter," John said with an uneasy demeanor. I knew all of John's tricks, but Melinda wasn't buying it. Neither was I.

"I don't know who you're talking about. But if you're here about Marion Whitlow's death, then like I said, call Sheriff Layton. He has all the details." God, I could love this woman.

"Um...Did you resay, Marion's dead?" He said my grandmother's name like he knew her personally.

"Yes. Now, I don't have time for this." Melinda began closing the door again, but John pushed harder because she inched back a step before gripping the door and wedged her foot on the other side of the door so as not to open further. "Step back from the door, Detective Vaughn, or I will call the sheriff myself, and you'll have a different kind of welcome to Dark Hollow Lake."

"Sorry. I have one more thing to say, and I'll leave," John conceded.

"What is it?" There was grit behind her words.

"Here's my card, with my new cell phone number on the back. When you see Chase, tell him I know who the killer is, and he's here in this town, and he's next." I heard the beat of his boots on the concrete steps as John walked away.

I whispered to Melinda, "Call the Sheriff." Then without thinking twice, I unchained the door and pulled open the door. "Who killed Cassie?" I called out to John.

The broad smile crossed the tired face I've known for most of my life as he turned around and faced me. The ease of his presence was absent. There was only tension-filled trepidation and frustration. My trust in this man waned to nil from the time I spent in this town.

"I knew you were here," John said, strain pinching the corner of his eyes.

"Who killed Cassie?" I pushed, not wanting to hear anything other than the name of the murderer.

"Marion." John flat out lied.

"That's not possible," I rebuked, knowing full well Marion couldn't physically harm a fly. She might have bullied some people, but that would be the end of it. I shook my head no. "There's no way. What's your proof?"

"Some of the leads I traced back to her and to this town. And your grandmother is the only one that is connected to you and Cassie." He took a step closer, but I didn't budge from my spot.

What's his excuse for the phone? "I tried to call you, but it was disconnected. Why is that, John?"

"I dropped my phone and had to get a new one."

I stepped out of the doorway with narrowed eyes and closed the door behind me, keeping Melinda inside. "And you couldn't keep the same number?" I asked with a frown, crossing my arms across my chest.

"Look, Chase—"

"No, John. What the hell is going on? I found out there was nothing out there about Cassie's murder. But what's strange is that my name showed up on the missing person list. Can you explain that to me?"

Crimson blotches rose on John's neck and cheeks. Just like his aura, the red was dominant, with a subtle shift of yellow telling me he was just as frustrated and possibly about to lie to me. Well, fuck him.

"I want straight-up answers from you," I spat, letting my anger show.

"I'll give you the straight answers, but not here. Can we go inside? It was a long ride coming here," John said as his eyes ran over the house with a quizzical stare.

"You knew about my grandmother all this time." I was far from comfortable bringing John into the house, especially with all the money Melinda and I discovered. Who knew how much more we hadn't found. What if he also learned about the money?

"Inside?" John pushed. I shook my head. "Then how about we go to the diner in town and talk," John suggested.

"Let me tell Melinda I'm going."

"Who is she?" John asked a single brow rose in question.

"Just a friend who's been helping me through this crap." I wasn't giving him any more, not until I knew I could trust him. But right then, something inside told me I couldn't—not with all the unanswered questions squirreling around in my head.

"I'll meet you in the car." John turned and headed back to his vehicle while I headed back inside.

"I called the Sheriff," Melinda whispered, her fingers clamped onto my arm.

"Make sure he has eyes on the diner."

"Is that where you two are going?" Melinda didn't look happy. "Maybe I should go with you."

"No. I don't trust John, not until I get all of the information from him, and I know he's not the killer. I want you to lock the doors and windows. Your job is to go through the boxes as much as you can and gather the money and put it somewhere no one can find it. Melinda, you're the only one I can trust."

"I have a bad feeling about this," Melinda said, not relinquishing my arm.

"I do too, but I need answers. That money is the root of all this shit. I just don't know where Cassie fits into all this, and I need to find out."

A tear slipped from Melinda's eyes. "Please be safe," she said before tugging me in for a hard hug. I returned the hug with one of my own and a gentle kiss on her lips.

"I will." With that, I grabbed my jacket and left, hoping what came next were answers I've been hoping for.

MELINDA

Through the curtained-off window, I watched Chase climbed into a black BMW. Once the vehicle was gone from my view, I made sure every window and door to the house was locked uptight.

I already called Layton's cell phone, which went straight to voice mail. "Please call back. A Detective Vaughn from Altoona came here. He knows Chase. They left for the diner. He wants you to meet him there."

I hung up, not feeling all that confident in Chase's plan. As I looked around the place, I realized if I had to leave this house, the money had to go with me. So I devised a plan.

I grabbed the boxes, Chase, and I already opened and brought them to what I thought was an office. Out of all the rooms, this one had no windows. Good for me since I had to do quick work if I had to leave in a pinch.

Quickly clearing off the large desk, I placed the boxes that were filled with money on top. Then one by one, from the pile Chase and I previously took boxes from, I opened them up and found more money.

Before I opened up any more boxes, I searched in Marion's closets and found several duffels of various colors and brought them back into the office. One by one, I began to fill the bags with the money. I tried to be as neat as possible, but it started to be overwhelming.

I barely made a dent out of three rows before I heard noises coming from the back door. I peeked in the kitchen, and the back door was being rattled. Someone was trying to break in. Then I saw a head bobbing up and down in the window, probably thinking they could climb through it. Thank god, Marion had enough sense to have small windows in the kitchen because the would-be intruder gave up that idea.

God forbid if they got in, how was I going to protect myself? *Think, Melinda.*

Remembering seeing the bat Chase brought from my house, I made a run for it. With the wood weapon in hand, my heart pounded furiously in my chest. I crawled on the floor so whoever was trying to break in couldn't see me.

As I checked the three deadbolts on the back door, I promptly appreciated Marion Whitlow's neuroticism before spying my cell phone on the kitchen table. Not caring if the person saw me this time, I grabbed the phone and called Layton again. This time he answered. As loud as my voice could carry, I shouted, "Sheriff Layton, I need you to get to Marion's place. Someone is trying to break into the house."

"I'll be right there. Stay on the phone with me. I'm texting Deputy Martin to head that way too." I could hear a muffled voice before the sounds of screeching tires. "Melinda, answer me." Layton's order cut through my alarm. "Are you alright?"

"Yes," I said as my panic started to drop. "I'm good.

Whoever it was, the would-be intruder took off," I said with absolute relief.

"Where's Chase?"

"He went off with that Detective Vaughn to the diner. Didn't you get my message?" I had to take a seat as my spent adrenalin left me slightly shaky and lethargic.

"I'm nearly there." He hung up, but I still clutched the phone to my chest.

Not two minutes later, Layton was pounding on the back door. "Melinda."

"Hold on." With the three deadbolts unlocked, I swung the door open and saw the sheriff slumped over slightly, hand on the house as if it was the only thing holding him up and huffing out heavy breaths. "Are you okay?" The last thing I wanted was for this man to die in from of me of a heart attack. The man might look like a healthy thirty-something male, but the slight bulge of his belly belied otherwise.

"I quickly checked the perimeter and saw no one," he heaved out more deep breaths and straightened. "Christ, I need to get my butt back in the gym."

"The guy must have heard me calling you because he took off in the direction of the falls. Sheriff, do you need a drink or something?"

"I'm fine." He brushed me off, but I could tell he wanted to rest. "It was a man?"

"Yes. Around six feet—maybe less. Slightly dumpy build. Black hair, like the man dyed it. Greasy. I couldn't make out his face well enough to give you details, but he was wearing a hunter's camo jacket and black jeans.

"That's enough." Layton grabbed his handset and radioed Martin to circle around Pine Road. The woods opened to the main road before it crossed into the Foxwood Manor territory. The eerie part of that neck of the woods was wrapped around the lake to the falls. I wasn't sure if it was the thought of that area that gave me the chill that ran down my spine or because of Jasper.

"I'm going to head back around and meet up with Martin. Keep the doors locked, and let me know if that guy comes back around. In the meantime, I'll send a deputy over to the diner. I need to have a word with Chase and that detective." The sharp stare he laid upon me conveyed just how serious he meant.

"I will." The second Layton drove out of sight, I closed and locked the door. I leaned against the heavy frame, my heart finally slowing to an even rhythm. I wasn't sure if I should call or text Chase on what happened, but no matter what, he needed to know someone tried to break it. And it so happened after he left the house.

I knew he needed to talk with his so-called friend, but this John is part of the murdering of good people and stealing money, then Chase had to know what he was dealing with.

I glanced over at the pile of untouched boxes and noticed Chase's wallet. I wasn't sure if he needed it, but I picked it up and opened it. I wanted to see Cassie's picture once again. But the moment I opened it, my fake card fell out and landed front side down.

I stared at the writing, and something struck me. *No, not something. The numbers.*

I ran to the entrance where I dropped John's card. I picked it up and eyed the numbers on the back. Then I rushed back to the room and compared it to my card.

"Holy crap. It's the same writing." I stumbled back, my knees knocking back into a stack of newspapers on the floor. "I have to call Chase. He's in danger."

With every punch of Chase's number, my breathing

sped up faster. But fear slashed me right down to the bone when the call went straight into voice mail. "Shit. Shit, shit. Chase, call me as soon as you get this message. John wrote the time, date, and place on my card. He is the killer."

26

CHASE

I wasn't what I was waiting for as the ride to the diner was quiet. I tried to wrangle all the questions in my head I wanted answers to, but I kept looking at John as though my silence was his cue to start talking.

Another mile under tires before my impatience kicked in. "Who killed Cassie, John?"

John glanced at me, eyes bloodshot like he hadn't slept for a while. "You won't believe me if I told you."

"Try me," I urged, keeping my voice even. The last thing I wanted was an argument, especially when the answers were within reach.

He blew out a long breath and stared straight ahead. "For you to understand why this person did what he did, I need to tell you from where all this started."

"I don't care, John. He took the one person I had left in this life away from me. Murdered an innocent woman who could never hurt a single living soul. A woman who loved butterflies. I just want the name." The strain in my jaw hurt from clamping my teeth too hard in that word.

John knew all this. I just thought…

"Chase, I know," he blurted, wetness from his eyes trailed down his cheeks. He wiped them away and began the tale of a person I didn't give a shit to know. "It was about twelve years ago, right before your mother...left. Your father and I, several agents from the APD task force, along with the DEA, had set up to bust a huge drug ring that ran out of New York that was connected to the DeMarcos family. It took two years, but we did it. We're talking heroin, cocaine, and several variations of drugs to choose from. But not only drugs, but there was money too. Tons of it."

"Money?" I echoed in question. Can it be? I kept silent and listened.

"Yeah. Well, several of us thought it wouldn't hurt to take a few bills. A few thousand here and there—It wasn't like anyone was going to miss it. But your father got greedy and took a million... or two."

"Now, why doesn't that surprise me?" I said, my voice loose, but my strangled nerves told me if my father was upfront and center in this scheme, there was more to it than just money.

"Me, your father, and three other officers—I won't mention their names were involved in taking more. The three officers involved had kids—a family. That money went for their schools and food on their tables."

John's justification for taking that drug money, especially the cops that had families, didn't ease the tension building in me. My mom, Cassie, and I never benefitted from any cash my father took. Henry must have hoarded his share for himself because our living conditions back then had never gotten better.

So far, everything John was telling me seemed to be the truth because his colors stayed blue mostly.

"How much did Henry actually stolen?" I asked, my

eyes never leaving John. Then a spike of yellow mixed in the blue, and red spread through his aura.

"Four point one million."

"Total?" I wasn't sure if I heard correctly. For some, four-point one million might be nothing. But from my standpoint, that money would have changed our lives for the better.

"Yes," John uttered under his breath.

My jaw went slack at his answer. "How much did you take?"

"About a million—but I never touched it. It is still hidden somewhere just in case."

"In case of what, John?" I was simply disgusted with the man. "How did you five take the money without getting caught?" I asked, completely oblivious that we were heading in the opposite way of town.

"Easy. There were over thirty million we confiscated, give or take a mill. With so much money, the DEA had no clue how much was actually confiscated. And no one really counted how much there was. Until..."

"Until what?"

"Until we found out for sure who the money belonged to because the DeMarcos made it damn fucking clear they wanted their money back. I guess they had some connections on the force, and someone snitched about the missing evidence."

I didn't like where this was going. My phone pinged with a voice mail, briefly shifting my attention, but I ignored it and focused on what John was confessing to.

"What happened after?"

"Retribution." That single word sent an icy chill up my spine. John continued on. "One by one, the cops that took part in the bust were dying. Your father and I figured we were next after one of the guys died in a mysterious fire."

"And the money?"

"I think whoever started the fire took it," he said with a note of worry. "After that fire, your father and I were the only ones left."

"And you think my father met his end the same way?" I asked, my eyes locked onto the man whose body went rigid. "John?"

"Your father..."

"What about my father?" The hard edge to my tone sliced through the air, making him wince. "Tell me."

"Henry thought that if he staged his death in a similar fire, he'd be free and clear of the DeMarcos," he rushed out.

"Are you saying my father isn't dead?" My voice rose an octave. "Is Henry still alive?"

"Chase, you have to understand. These people were gunning for us," John shot back.

"What about you? How did you fly under the radar?" I bit out. "Wait, I don't give a fuck. This whole fucking time, Henry has been alive while I've been struggling to take care of Cassie." I thought I hated my old man, but now? If he was still alive, I would kill him myself for what he put us through. What he had put me through. "Take me back. I'm done."

"I can't."

It was then I spied on the sign coming up telling us Sevier Bridge was up ahead. I stared wide-eyed and shocked. "You were the one that dropped the card...You killed Cassie."

"No. I'm telling you the truth. I promise you, Chase, I didn't kill Cassie. Her death was an accident." The swirl of raging colors around John told me he was telling me the truth but lying too. That didn't make any sense.

"Then what is the truth, John? Who killed..." the words drifted from my mouth as the truth smacked me hard across the face. That my dead father hadn't died in a fire, apparently he set up to fake his own death. And Cassie's died under John's watch. "Henry."

Like a spotlight on John's soul, his aura told me I hit the nail on the head.

Everything in me wanted to strike out, not caring if John retaliated. But something told me to stay still. Hold onto my anger. Keep in check.

Every molecule in my soul was being ripped out of my chest. Since the moment I found Cassie lying in a pool of her own blood, my life had been torn into shreds. "Tell me, damn it. Henry killed my sister?"

"I swear it. It was an accident."

Before I could scream at John, a figure stood several feet ahead, just past the bridge in an all too familiar manner. I began to shake with such fury that my fisted hands turned white. Acid heat rose from my stomach. I couldn't breathe. Couldn't talk. The last person I thought I'd ever see again was in Dark Hollow Lake. The car stopped right next to the man I had despised all of my life. Henry Bishop. My dead father was alive and well.

27

CHASE

The back passenger door whipped open, and my father slid right in, a nine-millimeter pointing at my head. My eyes fixed on the gun inches from my face while distaste ran across my tongue like rancid meat. My eyes met Henry's, at the gun and then back to him. "Hello, father," I said with an equal amount of disdain he was giving me.

"Hello, son." The sneer across his face was the welcome I expected.

I never lingered on the thought of who I looked like, but at that moment, I knew I was staring into a much older version of me. The same face, the same colored eyes I had seen in the mirror countless times. I remembered my mother used to say before church that I looked as handsome as my father. Her complement had made me on top of the world. But in those days, I was stupid and naïve about the world around me. Now, I was far from appreciative to see who I got my looks from.

Worn out like a battered tire on its last tread, Henry Bishop had seen better days. His hair at the root was gray, while the dye job barely covered the rest of the muddied color. Sweaty and disheveled, Henry looked like he'd been running a marathon through the woods.

I sat there, my body frozen in place, as the words tumbled out of my mouth. "You should have stayed dead."

"Really?" His disdain aimed a direct hit as the butt of the gun smacked me across the cheekbone. "Get moving, John." The slice of pain slashed across my face, and my brain was jarred from the impact. I touched my cheek as a trickle of warmth slid down my skin and came away with blood on my fingers.

"What the hell was that for?" John hissed in frustration as he took off, slightly squealing the tires. "That wasn't necessary."

"He's my son. I have every right," Henry spat out. "Now shut the fuck up and drive. I have the heat on me."

"What did you do?"

"What do you think I was doing? I checked the bitch's house, but someone called the cops, so I ran."

Was he talking about Melinda? Oh shit. I should have checked my phone. I bet it was her who was trying to contact me. While I contemplated my next move, they talked to each other like I wasn't even in the car.

"I told you to wait. Let me talk to Chase first," John ragged on as he passed a trailer park. A single glance at some of the dilapidated trailer homes, and I knew for certain James Randal wasn't a good landlord.

"Fuck you, John. If it wasn't for me, we'd have bigger problems," Henry snarled.

"Damn it, Henry. It's always about you." John's voice crested, causing me to slouch out of the pointed gun.

"Talk to me about what?" I asked, bouncing between the two men.

John let out an exaggerated breath. "Marion has something of Henry's."

The tightness at the center of my chest turned to concrete. That was it. The money in the boxes belonged to Henry.

"What is it?" I asked, playing stupid. There was no fucking way I wanted them—either of them to get their hands on the stolen money or let them know I knew about it. I didn't care if it belonged to the cartel or money-grubbing cops. My sister lost her life over this. I'd burn it first if I had to.

"The money you fucking idiot. I want the money." Henry bawled out, knocking the gun to the top of my head. The direct hit to my skull had me seeing stars, making my eyes tear.

I hunched forward, away from another probable blow to my head. For a blip of a second, I was going to round in on my old man, then I remembered the gun. I wouldn't put it past the bastard to shoot me. He killed one child. Henry wouldn't have any qualms shooting me.

"Jesus Christ, Henry. Sit your ass back, stop attacking Chase, and shut the fuck up. You got us into this shit. Now let me get us out of it. Again." John scolded with such censure that I knew he wasn't a willing party to this disaster. However, I still didn't trust him, mostly if he had covered up Cassie's murder to protect the piece of shit of a father. "Chase, are you okay?"

The caring tone in his voice had me looking at him with disbelief. "Am I okay? Do you think I'm fucking okay?" I slowly turned and faced the man next to me. I was afraid to speak my thoughts out loud with a grape-fruit-size lump in my throat but needed to know the truth. "Why did you kill Cassie?"

Henry swallowed hard. But those green eyes were void of any regret as his hand gripped the gun in a vise-like manner. "You want to know? Fine," he said flatly. Cold. So much so that I inwardly shivered at the chilly way he was staring at me. The fiery swirls of blue, red, and purple were shining like a beacon of evil. He was about to spill the truth.

"It was by accident," John repeated. There was no justifiable excuse for what Henry Bishop did to his daughter. No rational defense for killing a woman whose reasonings were that of a girl in a woman's body.

I ignored John and focused my energy on the son-of-a-bitch. "Why? Cassie was harmless." The raucous tone of my voice stabbed for blood.

"Was she?" That question caught me off guard. He continued. "Did you know that little bitch took my money and gave it to your grandmother? Fuck. I blame this on your worthless mother. Did you know your no-good mother left you to fend for yourself to find herself? All she took was the clothes on her back and a bottle of Jameson's for my troubles. That bitch had it coming to her when she died in the car accident a couple years ago."

"What?" Henry's ramblings of my mother scrambled my brain. "What are you talking about? What accident?"

"Never you mind," Henry relayed, with a thin smile as though he got one over on me.

"No. What do you mean she died a couple of years ago?" I looked at John, but he turned away from me. I wanted to punch off his face for being such a coward.

Henry was waving the gun around in the air like it was his baton. He continued on, ignoring my question. "Your sister did. In fact, she stole my money and gave it to that cunt of a grandmother."

First my sister and then my mother, and now my grandmother. "How did Cassie, who had ASD took your money and gave it to a woman we both didn't even know —or knew existed?"

"She did," Henry screamed while lunging forward, spittle sprayed from his words. He grabbed the top of my hair and roughly yanked my head back, pressing the gunpoint to my temple. "She confessed it to me right before she died." The crazed smile on his face was creepier than the woods I walked through coming here. "Did you know every time you left town, I had nice little chats with Cassie at John's house."

"I told you not to touch her." John swung his head around barked out, his tone hard like granite. "But you went too far."

Henry shoved my head forward, releasing my hair in the process. "You always pussy-footed around her, John. I got the job done—like fucking always. Besides, you wanted to know where the money was just as bad as I did. So quit your bitching. It's done."

Each word was a crushing blow to my heart. My poor sister had to endure so much, and I unwittingly was a part of her demise. Now I understood the state she came back to me whenever I came back home from out of state work. My eyes began to leak. I couldn't hold them back any longer. She never deserved to die, especially at the hands of her own father.

It took everything in me not to jump at the asshole. I didn't care if I got shot. Revenge was only in my mind. Before I could do anything, the car rolled to a stop right in front of Sevier mines entrance.

"We're here," John announced.

"What are we doing here?" I asked, but Henry pointed the gun at me.

"None of your fucking business. Just shut up and sit there. Your turn will come soon enough." Henry answered with indigence. He yanked my arm forward, over the front seat, and slapped handcuffs around my wrist. With the other half of the cuffs, he snapped around the steering wheel. "And if I see you get any bright fucking ideas and try to get out of this car, I'll plug you with so many holes, the coroner won't recognize you. Got it?"

What is stopping him now from doing it anyway? I thought but said nothing and simply gave him a curt nod.

Both men climbed out of the car and approached the mouth of the mine. All the while, Henry's eyes kept darting back to the car--to me. I wasn't going to stay put. I began my plans.

I was elated that Henry didn't take my phone because I climbed over the seat and centered myself in front of the steering wheel. I took out my cell, slumped down, and called Sheriff Layton.

"Damn it." The call went straight to voice mail. I left a message and then immediately dialed Melinda. By the second ring, she picked up.

"Oh, thank God. Are you all right." The tremor in her voice had me feeling bad for not answering her text sooner.

I'll apologize for it later. "Right now, I need you to find Layton. I'm at the Sevier mines with John and my father."

"What? I thought your father was dead," she squeaked out.

"So did I," I said with repugnance. My attention fixed on the two men standing in the mouth of the mine arguing with each other, then I saw it. A shadow. A third person, but I couldn't see who it was. They were standing inside the cave, away from the daylight.

"Layton just left. Chase, someone tried to break into the house." Fear resonated through the phone. "I thought..." she sucked in an audible breath.

"I know. It was my father," I angrily admitted. "He's been after the money all this time."

"Seriously? What a scumbag."

"That's not half of it," I added with reluctance. "My father killed Cassie. And somehow—I don't know, but my mother was also involved, but Henry didn't say." Admitting that out loud hurt more than I wanted to admit. Never in my wildest nightmares would I thought Henry—for all the nasty crap he had done in the past would be capable of doing vile things.

My stomach wanted to revolt, but I was too strung out from the raging vengeance still coursing through my veins.

"I'm so sorry, Chase." Melinda's remorse came out in a soft cry. "Why would a father do something so terrible to his kids?" I wished she was here with me. I need her warmth right about now. If I was in a different place, I'd laugh off the idea that I needed a woman like Melinda to bolster my strength. But in hindsight, I did. Melinda was the best thing that ever happened to run my ass over. And when this was all over, I had to reevaluate my life and see where life would lead me toward.

"I don't know, Melinda," I said with a growl. "It all comes down to that dirty money."

"Do you think he killed Marion too?"

Marion's death didn't even factor in until now. "As of now, I have no doubt." I straightened in my seat and said, "Get Layton and whoever he has out to the old mines. There are more than two people involved. But I don't know who and what is involved. Promise."

"I will."

With that, I hung up on her.

I focused all my energy on getting free from the cuffs. Opening up the glove box, I knew John might have a spare set of cuff keys handy. I quickly rummaged around until I found it. After I uncuffed myself from the steering wheel, I slowly got out of the car.

Glancing over at the entrance, I didn't see Henry or John anywhere near the mouth of the mine. Quietly as I could, I inched my way to the opening, leaving my ears to any voices.

Once I thought it was clear, I took several steps inside until the dark became too intrusive, and I couldn't see a damn thing. With my back to the girtered walls, I listened for John or my father's voice. Not a single sound was heard. I tapped the light app on my cell phone and followed the dirt path farther into the mine with caution.

Remaining plastered to the walls, I trailed the planked path while the light was cast down to the floor. When I came to a fork in the tunnel, I listened intently for any sounds or voices coming through both directions. To the right, I heard the faint echo of voices--John telling Henry to shut the hell up. I took a step in that direction until I saw the soft glow of light in the other tunnel. Then I saw him. The boy. He stood at the far end of the tunnel, an eerie glow around him, waving at me to follow.

I contemplated if I should go any further, but as the voices of Henry and John gotten louder, it gave me no choice but to head toward the boy.

Every step of indecision, the faint glow of light led me deeper into that tunnel. Several minutes past, when my cell phone blinked out. I stood in the pitch dark as fear began to bite at my senses like a hungry lion. For one second I stood stock still in the pitch black, and then the next, I knew my legs were swept from under me, and my head hit something hard. Pain so intense tore through my skull and rippled down my spine. I lost my breath, and blackness took over completely.

28

CHASE

I didn't know how long I laid there, but the pain in my head was evident enough that I might have a concussion. I sluggishly opened my eyes, but the dark I thought I'd be in was actually bright. Real bright. So much so that I had to use my hands to shield the light from my eyes.

"Chase." Melinda's voice came through as she blinded me with a light on her cell phone. "What happened?"

"I...Melinda?" I asked in confusion. My brain still rattled a bit. I winced at the pain from the base of my skull as I got on my unsteady feet. "Am I dead?"

A sorrowful chuckle rang from Melinda but was short-lived. "No, dang it. But I almost did. You scared the crap out of me, Chase. What happened? Who knocked you out?"

I paused for a moment; my thoughts rambled through my shaky memory as to what exactly did happen. "I followed John and Henry inside the mine and..." *The boy. I followed the boy, and then I fell—no, I must have tripped and hit my head. But that doesn't make sense.* "I guess I got lost, tripped on something in the dark, and hit my head. How did you find me?"

"I didn't. You were laying at the mouth of the mine like-like you were dragged out." The seriousness of her words had me stiffen.

My mouth dropped open at the virility of her words. "I think we need to get out of here," Melinda said as I leaned against her until we reached her car. "Where's your father and John?" she asked, slowly scanned our surroundings.

"I don't know where they are. But I think we do need to get out of here." Once I got strapped inside, I turned toward Melinda, who was chewing on her lower lip in worry. "Why did you come here? I told you to wait at the house."

"I couldn't just sit and wait. Are you sure you're okay?" Melinda asked again, pulling me in for a hug. "I swear, ever since you came into my life, I've had one scare after another. Why is that? What did I do to deserve this?" She tilted her face up to the darkening sky.

With a light squeeze back, I asked, "Did you see anyone here when you arrived? A car or a truck?" I didn't want to be blindsided again. However, I had a strange sensation that we weren't alone.

"No one was here, not even a car when I arrived. Chase, you still didn't tell me exactly what is going on." Melinda's slightly strident tone had me straighten a little more. Still not a hundred percent. Melinda opened the door and helped me inside the car.

"I tell you what I know as we head back to Marion's —Wait. The money," I rushed out, staring at Melinda with apprehension.

"Don't worry." The shy smile across her face sent relief through my body. "It's in a safe place," she said sheepishly. "All of ten bags worth."

"Ten? Well, I'm afraid to ask where, but I trust you," I replied, snagging her hand and squeezing it.

As we left Sevier's Mines and headed back to Dark Hollow Lake, the thought of Sheriff Layton popped into my head. "Why didn't you send Layton like I told you to?"

"I called him, but his cell went straight to voice mail again. I don't know what's with that man lately. I left a message on his cell and at the station."

We rolled through town, watchful for John's car. Then the thought hit me. They had to drive through town to get out. "Head to Randal's office. I have a feeling they're going to check that place out again."

"Are you sure?" The bleak look upon her face had me rethinking about the money.

"Tell me the money isn't in that office or at the house," I said, my eyes locked to her beautiful face.

"I promise you it's not in there or at Marion's. I told you the money is in a safe place," she reaffirmed, shaking her head at me. I relaxed at that news. "Chase, what are you going to do when we get there?"

"We need to catch them talking about Cassie's murder and of the money they stole."

The car suddenly stopped. "You can't go in there. You're injured. How are you going to defend yourself if they see you?" she argued. "You need to call Layton and leave it the police hands."

I let out slow even breaths, hoping my vision stopped spinning. "I'm okay." I insisted on the lie. *Maybe a little whiplash.* But I didn't say that, but I kept on. "Besides,

I'm going to call Layton myself and tell him to get his ass to Randal's."

"I don't believe you." Her aura swirled with worry and anxiety. "You're in pain—I can see it across your face right now." Melinda was right, but I wasn't going to fess up.

"Look." I took her hand and squeezed it gently. "I mean it, I'm fine. A little shaken, but that is all. I know you don't like the idea of me going in there, but someone has to make sure to keep an eye on those two sons-of-bitches, until Layton grabs them."

"But you said they're dangerous."

"They are, especially my father. He's desperate and unpredictable enough to do anything to get that money. And that's why I have to do this. I need to stop them. Henry especially."

"Please explain to me the severity of this situation again." Her fingers tightened around mine like a vise.

"If my father can kill his only daughter, I don't see him having any trouble torturing me or you to get the location of that dirty money. If my father was telling the truth about my sister's involvement, and there's proof of what Henry did, I'm even more driven to make sure you're safe, and the money is put into proper hands, with Henry and John in jail for a long, long time."

A sour taste ran across my tongue at the idea that sister had anything to do with this ordeal. Then the thought of my mother came into play. What Henry off-handedly said in the car confused me to the point that I didn't know what to believe out of that asshole's mouth.

"Chase." Melinda's voice drew me out of my dour thoughts.

"I have to do this for Cassie. I owe it to her." The

ache in my chest wrenched tighter at the loss of my sister: Cassie and her dancing butterflies.

We stayed idle for a few more minutes before Melinda finally put the car into drive.

Not surprisingly, John's car was parked right in front of the real estate office. We pulled up a few buildings down, and my thoughts went to Randal's ghost. I hoped that I didn't have to see him again, but I doubted it. The man was angry, and I knew why. He was murdered. The question was, how was Randal involved in this twisted situation.

"I really wish you weren't going in there," Melinda explained, a significant hitch of worry in her words.

"I think Randal's death is another link to my father, Melinda," I said, her face paling at my admission. "I think my father had a hand in his accident. And if that's the case, Randal must have also been connected to the money Henry had stolen. Though, I'm only speculating."

"With everything that has gone on, I believe it." Melinda shivered, rubbing her hands across her arms.

"I'm going to call Layton. Hopefully, he'll answer this time." Again the sheriff's call went into voice mail. Either it was too much of a coincidence that La wasn't answering his cell, or something else was happening in Dark Hollow Lake. I had to believe in the latter. "I can't wait for the sheriff. I need to get in there now."

"Okay." The sullen resolve was evident in Melinda's eyes as she started to chew her lower lip. "Just be careful, Chase, because if you get hurt, I don't know what to do. So please."

I found her ramblings endearing and cute.

A smile tipped my lips as I reached out and caressed her cheek. "Melinda." She aimed her pretty blue eyes at me. A spark of need to protect this woman shot through my fingers as I caressed her cheek. I opened my mouth to tell her how I felt, but the words were lodged in my throat. There was so much respect, appreciation, and feelings of like—no, not like, more than the friendship I wanted from her. But this wasn't the time to express it. Who knew the start of this journey I'd be falling for a girl who nearly ran me off the road. But here, I did not want to leave her side. Instead, I leaned in and kissed her solemnly until her arms wrapped around my neck and pressed tighter against me.

Who knew how long we stayed that way, but my only purpose was to assure Melinda that everything would be all right.

I slowly pulled away and stared into her calming blue eyes. "I'll be safe. Promise."

"Okay," she uttered in a sigh. I couldn't help myself. My eyes strayed down to her appealing lips again. In case anything happened to me, I leaned in and kissed her once more. I lingered. She let me. As I pulled back, I saw disappointment across her face. I knew she wanted more. And I wanted to give it to her.

"Stay here."

"Wish you would too," she replied as she glanced out the window to the dark building.

"Melinda, if my feeling is correct, and they are looking for only the money, then we are good. Now, I have to go," I said, but she had a tight grip on my jacket.

"Please be safe," she said once more and kissed me with fierce determination. I took what she was offering and reveled in it.

I pulled back and got out of the car.

I checked the front door and found it locked. With hand gestures, I told Melinda I was heading to the back of the building. Sure enough, the lock was busted off, and the back metal door was partially ajar.

With utmost care, I slowly opened the door and slipped inside. The back room was filled with boxes on top of boxes. It reminded me of Marion's house. I bypassed the stacks, trying not to topple any of the boxes as I made my way to the front end of the office.

Noises and soft muffled voices reached my ears from the second floor. They were arguing, which didn't surprise me. My father was the biggest asshole. He never listened to anyone, especially to John or when Henry thought he was right.

Keeping my ears to their bickering, I took each step with caution while watching for any activity on the second floor. The last thing I wanted was to notify them of my presence or had to deal with Randal's ghost. When I reached the top, noises came from the office to the right. I crept along the wall, just outside the room and took out my cell, and hit the voice memo app to record.

"I knew the second you told that bitch about the money, it was going come back and bite me in the ass," Henry screeched.

"She was your wife. I assumed she'd be happy with the situation. Hell, Henry, I thought the shit hole you had your family living in would have been an incentive to get on board with the plan. How was I to know all this time? Barb knew where the money was and gave it Marion," John said with strife.

Mom? She was the one who actually took the money? It didn't make any sense. But I kept listening.

"Maybe I shouldn't have punch Marion that hard— but that bitch wouldn't tell me where the money is. And now she's dead, and it's all your fucking fault," My father yelled so loud that I wouldn't be too surprised the next building over hadn't heard his shouting.

"If you listened to me, we wouldn't be in this mess," John shouted back with vehemence.

Henry threw something. The crash made me jump away from the wall, giving me perfect viewing of the room they were in. I quickly saw John bent over, his hand to his mouth, blood dripping down his chin, and the floor.

Anger plastered on his face, John straightened and charged at Henry. He grabbed my father by the neck and slammed him to the wall. "Listen to me, you asshole. You didn't have to kill Marion or Cassie for that fact. She was innocent in all this time. And stop blaming me for your fuck up. If you did what I said to do back then, we would not be in this mess."

"Turning the money over to DeMarco would have been a death sentence for me. You know it. Either way, I was dead." Henry wheezed out.

"And so is your daughter by your hands, and we can't get her back." The ferocious frown on John's face said it all. He released Henry and stepped back. "Cassie's death is on you. Along with Barbara's and Marion's too."

"All three were worthless," Henry coughed out, his hand at his throat.

I wanted nothing more than to blast inside that room and kill Henry myself. Cassie wasn't worthless, and neither was my mom. But John was right. They were dead, and I couldn't do anything to bring them back. I pushed down the hollowed-out burning feeling that nested in my chest and let the frustration coursed through me instead.

I wanted to jump into the room, but a dark cloud

emerged through the corner of the room. I knew immediately who it was. J. Randal.

I hardly had time from the moment Henry and John saw the apparition to them running out of the room in sheer terror. I raced to the next room that held office furniture and hid behind the door. The men barreled past me, pounding footsteps down the stairs, with the clatter of furniture echoing off the walls in the hallway. And then silence.

I snuck out from my hiding place and glanced down the staircase to be sure they were gone. I headed into the office and stopped dead. Randal was hovering over his desk with an expectant look on his scary face. I didn't move or breathe, afraid of what he might do. I never connected with the dead before, so this was new for me.

Randal's gaunt eyes honed in on me. With grim determination on his face, he pointed a finger toward the top left-hand drawer of his desk. I glanced at where he was directing me to. Finally dawned on me what he was doing. Randal was helping me.

With a slow nod of understanding from me, he pasted on a serene smile that made him look even almost human, and then he evaporated into thin air.

I waited for a beat or two, making sure Randal left for good. I then proceeded to open the drawer he was referring to. There were pens, pencils, and assortments of office supplies one would typically have. I moved things around and found nothing unusual. I was about to close the drawer when I spotted a partially hidden key wrapped in a piece of paper with a rubber band binding them together.

I picked up the key and unraveled the rubber band and paper. The key looked normal. Nothing odd about it. Silver and notched. But what was on the paper threw me.

It was the same date, time, and where to meet written on the card I found on Cassie's body.

I took a step back, unbelieving what I was seeing. This wasn't a coincidence. I took another step back and knocked my elbow into the filing cabinet. Pain shot through my funny bone that my eyes began to water. Realizing I dropped the key, I bent over to pick it up when I noticed a lock at the bottom drawer of the cabinet.

It was strange to see a lock so low like it was done on purpose. Staring at the key and then the cabinet, I decided why not. I kneeled down, stuck the key inside, and twisted it. Sure enough, the key turned with ease, and the bottom door popped open.

There were ledgers—at least ten deep inside it. I grabbed one and glanced inside it. Numbers. Lots of it. But I couldn't make out what they were for. Though, it didn't matter. I was made sure to grab them all. "Maybe Melinda could make sense of it." Then I spotted blueprints and grab those too.

Not bothering to look further, I headed out, leaving through the front door.

I saw Melinda wide-eyed as she started the car. With an armful of ledger books and the blueprint, I climbed into the car and said, "Your house. We have some studying to do."

29

MELINDA

"What am I looking at?" I asked, scanning the hundreds and hundreds of numbers in what looked like business ledgers. "These numbers don't make any sense. But these might be codes to what those numbers mean."

Chase scanned the book I had in my hand and then his. "It doesn't make sense None of them do. But I have a feeling you're right about lettering on the side of each log as codes. We just don't know what the codes are." He picked up a couple other ledgers on the kitchen table and opened them up. "What if these numbers are money amounts."

"But from where?" I asked, placing the book down on the table and went to refill my coffee cup, stopping midway as an idea popped into my head. I spun around and faced Chase. "I wonder if Randal was mixed in some nefarious stuff, like money laundering and such."

Chase shot out of his seat, one of the ledgers in his hand. "You might be right. But I have a feeling John or my father might know the answer to that."

"Speaking of those jerks. I wonder where they ran off to. I swear there was a fire under their feet when they tore out of the building and got into their car," I said with a chuckle.

"Forget about them for now. I want to know about the ledgers and what this blueprint is for," Chase said as he took everything off the table and spread the blueprint across the surface.

I took a much closer look and realized what I was looking at. "It's the old Sevier mobile home park and abandoned Sevier mines and the land surrounding it. Now, why would Randal have this?"

A knock on the front door drew our attention immediately, which quickly made me panic. Chase shoved the blueprint and pointed to the ledgers. "Hide them."

As he took his time to answer the door, I shoved all the books back into a bag and immediately stashed them and the blueprint in my bedroom closet. I took a couple deep breaths to calm my racing heart and casually walked out to see who came to call.

I found Sheriff Layton standing in the kitchen. "Sheriff," I said, not surprised to see him. I'd called a hundred times, but who was counting.

"Melinda." He took off his hat, eyes weary as he looked at me. "I'm sorry that I couldn't call back in time. There was a bad situation at the Foxwood Manor that needed my full attention. We're short-handed and such—"

"Sheriff came by to tell us that Marion's house was ransacked," Chase interrupted. The calm in his voice contradicted the fiery anger in his eyes.

We both knew there would be a good possibility his father and John were going back to Marion's to look for the money. "How bad?" I asked the dour-faced lawman.

"Let's just say the entire house was ripped apart. It was like they were searching for something mighty important."

Chase glanced at me, his face resolute. I gave him a nod before turning the Layton. "We know what they are looking for."

Layton eyed me and then at Chase. "What would that be?"

"Money. Lots of it," Chase said bluntly.

"Stolen money," I added.

Layton's eyes narrowed. "Might as well sit a spell." He took a seat and pulled out this notebook. "Start from the beginning."

Chase explained everything. From when he got here to how his father was a dirty cop and that he and his fellow officers acquired the money from a major bust that happened years ago. He repeated what John confessed about how much money was taken and who it belonged to. It was all fascinating, like reading an exciting crime novel. Though, I would never utter those words to Chase. He had lost so much in his life that telling the man I had come to care about that his messed up life was exciting.

"Please tell me again about your sister's involvement," Layton said in a kinder tone. "And how much money are we talking here?"

"I don't know the exact amount. Only what John told me. Sheriff, my sister didn't take the money. She was way too young at the time," he explained. "I was almost fourteen, and Cassie was barely nine at the time of the bust. Besides, Cassie had Autism Spectrum Disorder, her mind didn't work the way we do. There was no way she devised a plan to steal that much money—or steal anything, period."

"So your mother took the money and gave it Marion for safekeeping."

"From my understanding, yes, with my grandmother's help. Though some things didn't add up," Chase confided, his eyes welling up with tears. "I'm sorry, but this whole situation is bringing up..."

I went to Chase and pulled him into a tight hug. "I'm here. It's going to be okay," I whispered.

The appreciation shined in his beautiful green eyes. "Thanks."

Layton cleared his throat, catching our attention. "So Marion was involved," Layton said with an exhausted breath out.

"Yes. We found an ungodly amount of money stashed in Marion's house."

"Don't forget Randal, if we're telling him everything," I said to Chase.

"What about Randal?" There was grit to Layton's words. There was no doubt the sheriff hated that man.

"We think he was money laundering for someone, but we don't know who. We found a bunch of ledgers with some big money amount on them and a blueprint. Though there were no names on the books, and the blueprint is of the mobile park and old mines," I explained.

"Well, that explains a lot," Layton grunted.

"What?" I asked with curiosity.

"The blueprint. Randal had always got it in his head that he would change the town into a full resort—to match the other side of the lake. I always wondered why he was gobbling up property in and around town when he barely sold a house or two for the past year. I think some of that money was his hands, and that's how he was able to purchase those properties."

"Where Randal was concerned, I'm not surprised to hear that," I admitted with a huff.

"I can't be sure on that since my father and John didn't mention Randal," Chase admitted with a shake of his head.

"Where are the ledgers?" Layton asked as he looked to Chase.

"With the money," I lied, my eyes straying to Chase, who gave me a slight nod of approval.

Layton nodded. "Well, the DeMarco family..." Layton paused, tapping the table with his index finger in thought. "Now that's a dangerous bunch. Seems like Henry Bishop is still in a pickle even though it's been more than ten years since the bust. Taking DeMarco's money and then faking his death was a ballsy move on your father's part. However, the DeMarco family is still very active in the criminal world. If any of them finds out that Henry's still alive and in here in Dark Hollow Lake?" Layton shook his head with dismay. "We're going to have some very unsavory people come around these parts and stir up some major trouble," Layton grated out with a grim frown. "I think the ledgers, the blueprints, and the money should be in the hands of the law. Where's the money?"

"I put it in a safe place," I said, my eyes shifted over to Chase, who gave me a knowing smile. He didn't want me to reveal where the money was hidden to Layton. "Chase doesn't even know where I put it."

"I don't think it's a good—"

"I don't trust anyone, Sheriff." Chase cut him off. "If Melinda said it's in a safe place, then I believe her."

"Okay..." Layton looked at me and continues. "I can't agree, but I guess I don't have a choice in the matter or the time to argue. If you say the money is safe, I believe you both. Now, my next concern is to track down Henry Bishop and John Vaughn. We can deal with the money and the rest then. In the meantime, I have to inform DEA and Altoona PD on this matter since it started in their jurisdiction." Layton got up and turned to me. "Melinda, if you know the money is safe, then do me a favor and stay away from it. The last thing I want is for you to be in a hostage situation." He then asked Chase to walk him out.

I took Sheriff Layton's advice to heart, but I wasn't sure if I could stay away from my house since I stowed the bags in my cellar. A raw nervousness at what could happen hit me hard. I knew it might have been stupid to bring the money here, but it was the safest spot I could think of.

It wasn't long before Chase came back in, a pensive look on his face. "What did he say?" I asked, touching his arm. I yearned for that connection.

He wrapped an arm around me. It was instinctual like he knew I needed his touch—his reassurance that everything would be okay.

"He wants us to remain here while he and his officers track down Henry and John."

"Then we'll wait," I muttered under my breath, feeling the warmth of his skin.

"But what do we do in the meantime? I'm too damn antsy to sit and do nothing," he said as he studied the floor for the answers.

My cheeks heated up at the salacious image I had in my head of what I wanted to do. "I can think of one way of keeping busy." I gathered my courage and glanced up at Chase's face. His frown turned into a wicked grin that melted my trepidation away. He tightened his arms around me at the same time I brought him down for a greedy kiss.

Yeah, good plan.

30

CHASE

I wasn't sure what time it was, but I could see the moon partially obscured by dark clouds through Melinda's bedroom window. Cocooned in the warmth of Melinda's arms, her breathing was even.

I gazed across her serene face, to her well-kissed lips, and wondered what I did I do to deserve her in my life. I thought my lot in life was to care for my sister Cassie. I always worried about the next paycheck and ensured we didn't go hungry and have a roof over our heads.

All my life, I never thought to have someone who would care for me in a deserving way. But here I was, holding on for dear life and afraid that everything I cherished now was to disappear on me, all because I didn't deserve it. Melinda showed me in such a short amount of time that I was deserving of love.

I ran headlong into this fucked up mess with only one purpose in mind, to find Cassie's killer. Instead, I found a beautiful woman who trusted me enough to help me, a grandmother I barely got to know, a shit ton of money that wasn't mine, and the truth about my father.

"What are you thinking about?" Melinda asked with a kiss on my jaw.

"Thought you were asleep." My attention shifted back to her with a sated smile on my face.

"You're evading my question," Melinda said as she wrapped around my middle and snuggled in.

I kissed the top of her head. "Just thinking that it's been a week from hell, and I can't think of any other place but here, in this bed with you."

A blush bloomed on her cheeks as she wiggled even closer to me. "I know. Crazy?"

"Crazy isn't the word."

"Tell me about Cassie."

"She was beautiful inside and out. Even though she didn't talk much, Cassie conveyed so much in her actions."

"Like what?" Melinda rested her head on my shoulder.

"She loved to dance. As far back when she was about six, I could remember she used to dance about the house with my mother's smock on. She said she was dancing like her butterflies. She did love her butterflies," I chuckled, remembering the last time she did that.

"Butterflies?"

"Yes. Actually, only one butterfly in particular, but I can't think of the name. It was her favorite thing in the world. She drew it with markers or painted it at her enrichment class."

"What's the colors?" Melinda asked as she rubbed her nose across my neck.

"The wings are the color of dark maroon with blue

dots—you know she told me once the reason why the butterflies dance?

"Why?"

"It's because they're sad... Um, I never understood what Cassie meant by that," I admitted, stroking her silky skin on her arm.

"Dancing because they are sad," Melinda repeated, absently tracing her fingers around my nipple, which was doing wicked things to my body.

I pulled her hand away from my chest and pressed my hardening length against her. "Stop doing that, or I'll do dirty things to you," I demanded, taking possession of her mouth. As I delve deeper, I heard an odd sound like clinking glasses. Melinda also froze, listening with intent. There it was again.

"Was that glass breaking? Dang it. Caleb just fixed that back door," Melinda whined in a whisper.

"Call the cops," I ordered, and told her to stay put.

I slipped out of bed and grabbed the bat Melinda brought back from Marion's house.

I carefully opened the bedroom door and crept out to the hallway, and listened more intently. More noises, like breaking glass, became evident as I got closer to the kitchen.

My bad feelings rarely failed me, and right now, I had the sense that the people breaking into Melinda's house were my father and John.

I barely made it to the kitchen when I saw John crossing over the slider's shattered glass in the kitchen.

"John," I said with so much disdain that I must have caught him off guard.

"Chase—No Henry," John screeched. The blow to the back of my shoulders landed before I got a chance to react. Pain exploded across my spine, which had me jerking sideways in the other direction before crashing down onto my knees. Henry landed another hit to my back, and I face-planted onto the wood floor.

"Don't be a pussy, John," Henry spat, leaning close to me with a gun in his hand, pointing it at my face. "The boy isn't dead… yet. Go get that bitch."

"You son-of-a-bitch," I slurred, hoping Melinda heard the commotion so she could hide. "I already called the cops." I slowly got to my knees as Henry stuck the gun in my face.

"I bet you didn't," Henry said in a brittle tone. "John, I told you to grab that bitch. Now, boy, where's my fucking money?"

"I don't know what you're talking about." I glared at the man who never got a clue how to be a good father or a good man.

He back-handed me across the face. I tasted blood immediately and spat at his feet. "Don't be stupid like Randal, Chase. Just give us the fucking money, and we'll go away."

"What do you mean, like Randal?" I had to keep him talking to give Layton time to get here if Melinda reached him in time. I slowly rose to my feet and faced down the man that never gave a rat's ass about me.

"Randal got greedy with my money. So with a little push," he snickered, using his hands to show me how he killed Randal. "I got rid of him for good. Now stop fucking around. Tell me where the money is, and we'll leave you alone so you can go play house with your slut."

John walked back in with Melinda in his grips. Her face was chalky white, eyes wide with fearful tears.

"Why?" Pushing Henry was the wrong thing to do. He had a short fuse when things didn't go his way. I didn't want him to go half-cocked to get that gun away from him, especially if Melinda could get hurt.

"Why what?" Henry growled, a deep v formed between his eyebrows. He pushed the tip of the gun to my forehead.

"Why keep us alive when I know all about the shady shit you and John did in the past? Or that you killed your own daughter, Marion, and Randal for some dirty drug money? You never had a single merciful bone in your body? So why now?"

The man laughed—actually, a full-on belly laugh. For a brief moment, he pulled the gun back and then swiftly aimed it at Melinda. A squeak of horror eked out of her as the gun was trained on her.

"Don't move, baby," I whispered to Melinda, who stood frozen on the spot.

"How sweet," Henry mocked, but my attention shifted to John as he stared down at the floor in silence while my father got his jollies off.

Finally, John looked at me, eyes full of tears, which surprised me. He opened his mouth as though he was about to say something but clamped his lips tight. I shook my head at him. Anger, disappointment, and regret coursed through my veins at John. I thought I could trust the man, but John's deceit was too great to ever forget.

For so long, I looked to him as a father figure. But now, his betrayal was just another stab to my heart.

I averted my attention back to Henry, who stopped laughing and was now glaring at John and then at me. "What? Did you think you were going to get help from this asshole?" Henry let out another chuckle before pressing the muzzle of the gun back to my forehead. "Remember, boy, that money is also his. I might have killed Cassie, but John, dump your precious sister's body in Lake Altoona so no one will ever find it."

A cry of anguish tore from my throat at the thought of Cassie's body being dumped carelessly away like some no-good trash. I wanted to get up and kill the two, but the gun Henry jammed into my forehead hindered my attempts. I needed to rail in my rage for Melinda. She was now my main reason to stay alive.

"I'm not the only one in the wrong here, Chase. Ask your father what he did to Barbara." I wanted to ask why dredge up my mother's name, but the look of murder veiled over Henry's eyes.

"What about my mother?" I hissed, posing the question to Henry directly.

"Fucking Christ, you couldn't leave well enough alone." He turned the gun on John and shot him in the chest.

I swung hard across his face, catching Henry off guard, and knocked the gun out of my old man's hands. I landed blow after blow across his face until he dropped to the ground. But I didn't stop. It was all Henry's fault. "You will pay for their deaths," I screamed.

Just as I was about to let loose another punch, an arm wrapped around me and dragged me off of my bloody father. Still red with rage, I fought my capture until Melinda's voice cut through my mania.

"Chase." Her beautiful but tear-filled eyes erased my anger. I slumped back against Layton, who was steadying me. Melinda rushed into my arms, cries of worry streaked down her face. "Are you okay?" she whispered into my chest.

"I will be," I uttered, meaning it. But my eyes were fixed on John, who was holding his bloody chest, his hazy stare filled with remorse.

"Ambulance is on its way," One of Layton's deputies said to John as they pressed down on the bleeding wound. As for the two other officers that rushed in, they grabbed Henry, hauled up onto his feet, and handcuffed him. He relented easily.

"Give me a second." I kissed the top of Melinda's head before she released her stranglehold around my middle. As the cops relayed the Miranda rights to Henry, I walked to John. "Did you ever care for us?"

"I-I loved you kids like my own." John rasped out in a painful cry, his eyes filled with tears. "I'm sorry..." He didn't finish. John didn't have to. There was nothing he could say to make up for what he did to Cassie and to me.

Yet, I had plenty to say to Henry. I turned to my father with this. "I hope you rot in jail for the rest of your life knowing you didn't win." With that, I walked away.

"Are you ready?" Melinda asked solemnly. Her black dress clung to her shapely form as she slipped into her black heels.

"As ready as I'll ever be." I smiled sadly down at her, in the black suit I wasn't used to wearing.

The month had been tumultuous, to say the least, but we were finally here. Combatting the sullen mood of the day was hard to do. But ultimately, on this sad day, I was burying my sister Cassie.

With Melinda's help, she set up my sister's funeral at the church in town. The wake was going to be tiny. There was nobody to be shown since Cassie had to be cremated after an autopsy was done. I was upset at first because I wanted to say a proper goodbye to my sister. But I understood why with the amount of deterioration of her body, it was for the best.

Melinda told me I had to look at today as a celebration of the life my sister had. She was right. I couldn't stay focused on Cassie's death anymore. I needed to honor my sister by remembering how she lived her life to the fullest.

I reached for Melinda and wrapped her in my arms. "Did I say thank you for all this?"

"You did, and you're welcome. Now let's get a move on." She poked at my stomach before picking up her purse and headed out the door.

I stared at the woman I was falling in love with day by day and wondered what I would have done without her this past month. Melinda was my bright star in my worthless life. She'd been there from the time she almost killed me with her car to now. I chuckled, thinking of what kind of stories I would tell my kids and grandkids about how Melinda and I had met.

As for Henry and John? The prosecutors in Pennsylvania and Tennessee pooled their invaluable efforts and sent both men to prison for a long time.

Henry got life for killing James Randal because the asshole video taped himself pushing James down the stairs. With John's help, the prosecutors had enough evidence on Cassie murder. With the scar left behind from Henry's ring, Marion's death was against Henry too. With the other charges built against Henry, I had a feeling that no amount of appeals would get his sorry ass out of jail.

As for John, he barely survived the gunshot and was sentenced to twenty-five years for aiding and abetting Henry, with a few other charges on top of that. He got a plea bargain since he spilled the beans about everything from taking bribes to the DeMarcos raid and the reason for Henry faking his death. John also explained what kind of deal they had with Randal, who used to do the books for the DeMarcos family. How convenient, wasn't it? As for the blueprints, the three were in on it developing the bought properties and turn Dark Hollow Lake into a bigger resort town. Grand plans went all downhill when Randal got greedy.

Henry did confess that Randal had threatened to expose Henry to the DeMarcos if he didn't cough up more money. So Henry killed Randal to silence the man. Layton informed me that the DeMarcos were under investigation, and all of the money and the ledgers recovered by Melinda and me was handed over to the Feds.

However, I still didn't understand how and exactly when my mother got a hold of the money and gave it to Marion. John said my mother's involvement was minor, but the timeline didn't make sense. I figured that secret was buried with my mother because I would never visit my father for the answers

Right before we got into Melinda's car, the mailman walked up with an envelope package. "Chase Bishop," he called out, extending me the parcel.

"Who's it from?" Melinda asked as she reached my side.

"I don't know." I took the package and thanked the old mailman. We head back into the house to open it. "There's no name or return address."

I grabbed my buck knife off the table and sliced open the package. I looked inside and then dumped out the contents onto the table. There was a ruby gold necklace I remembered belonging to my mother. A man's wedding ring, a key to a safe deposit box, and a letter. I caressed the pendant before turning my attention to the letter.

I picked it up and scanned the bottom to see who wrote it, and I froze. "It's from John," I uttered in disbelief and dropped it. "I can't read it."

"Chase, there has to be a reason why he sent you all

this," Melinda said as she, too, touched the necklace. "It's pretty."

"It belonged to my mother." I picked I up and said, "Turn."

"No, that's—"

"No arguing, woman," I ordered with a smile.

She did as I asked, and I placed the necklace around her neck and linked it closed.

Melinda stroked the stone. "I'll cherish it forever," she said, her eyes filled with adoration. She then picked up the letter. "Do you want me to read it?"

I nodded, not able to get the words out. Each syllable was clogging my throat.

Dear Chase,

I hope you find this letter as the truth of what happened to your mother. I wanted your father to tell you, but he's too far gone from the fact. It was he who drove your mother away from you and Cassie. His bitterness, jealousy, and selfishness tore your family apart.

The truth is, your mother never died when you were fourteen. She died two years ago from a drunk driving accident she caused in that town, killing a family of three and herself.

I'm sorry, son, that you had to find out this way. I wanted to tell you a thousand times that she was alive and watched over you whenever she could. But your father tormented her and me from expelling the truth. With the help from a few friends, Henry made sure she never came around and exposed you kids to the truth. Even after your father faked his own death, he refused to let your mother take care of you. Now you know.

Barbara wanted Cassie to have her necklace and her father's ring for you. The key is to a safe deposit box.

The contents inside are yours. Do what you want with all of it.

I'm sorry.
John

I wasn't sure if I was still breathing when Melinda finished reading John's letter. It was like I lost my mother all over again with the truth of her life not ending until two years ago. I wasn't sure if I was angry or sad at the news. Maybe numb, after all, that had happened. Melinda, who stood there, quietly dropped the letter onto the table. She shook her head, eyes brimming with tears.

"What's wrong?"I asked, taking a step her way, but she shook her head no, putting a hand out to stop me. Then John's word hit me like a bulldozer.

"Your mother." She swallowed hard and continued. "She was the one who killed my family." That statement stung like a bat to my head. I wanted to deny it, but I knew what she was saying was true.

"I'm sorry." I reached her side before she crumpled in on herself. "I'm so sorry, baby."

I held onto her so tight as though our souls couldn't live without each other. I wiped away every tear and tried to kiss away the pain my family had caused her. "I promise I'll do whatever it takes to make it up to you," I said with a solemn vow.

Her watery eyes met mine with surprise. "You have nothing to be sorry for, Chase. You didn't kill my family. So please don't say that." She pulled out of my arms and grabbed some tissues. She blew her nose and wiped her eyes clear. After a moment, she said, "Today is for you, and for Cassie. Okay? We'll talk about this later," she uttered in a sniffle.

I didn't care if we were late. I pulled Melinda back into my arms and held her until I knew she was on steady ground. "I don't know how I got so lucky to have you in my life."

I didn't know how long we stood there, but I'd stay forever to make her happy.

We finally made it to the church. Surprisingly there were several cars parked in the lot. Before I took the first step into the church walkway, I spotted a small group of butterflies hovering over an open grave. Something urged me to check it out.

"Give me a second," I said to Melinda as I walked past the small iron gate that separated the graveyard to the main yard.

As I approached the flock of butterflies, they flitted away. Yet, they remained cloistered together in the air like a kaleidoscope of flatting wings.

I took another step, fixed on the colors of their wings. The design looked familiar, and I immediately remembered where I saw them. It was in Cassie's room. These were the butterflies she was obsessed with and insisted they were special. Chase, you know my butter-flies like to dance even though they are sad. I remembered Cassie saying. *"You're right, Cassie. They do dance."* A bloom of emotions filled my chest. I tried to breathe in the calm, but it was hard when every pent-up feelings wanted to surge forth and blast me from this universe.

"They're called the Mourning Cloaks, but the folks around here sometimes call them the death butterflies," a man beside me said sagely. "It's funny. They look like they're dancing in the air."

I turned to look at the man. "Death butterflies?" I asked, glancing down at the bible in his hand. The colors around the man had me drawing in a breath. I took a slight step back from him as the muted colors of blue, purple, and grey took me back. There were thin slashes of black mixed in too, which gave me extra pause. These were warning colors I had come to know. Yet, with the constant changing, I could be reading the man wrong.

"Yes. I've only seen them out and about when someone is about to be buried or had died." His admission reminded me of what Cassie had said. *They dance when they're sad, Chase.*

"That's strange," I uttered, but my eyes automatically trained on Melinda, who was walking toward us.

"Not for around here," he replied with a pleasant smile.

"Chase." Melinda gave me a weary look. She wrapped an arm around my waist and squeezed. "You met Pastor Wesley Johnson. He's doing the eulogy today," she explained. Her attention shifted to the butterflies. "Wow. I never saw that before."

"It's nice to finally meet you, Chase. Even under these dower circumstances." The pastor stuck out his hand. I hesitated but took his hand, even though I was suddenly wary of the man. His aura spiked in various colors, mainly green the second his hand grasped onto mine. He was hiding something. I knew it but wasn't sure what.

I quickly dropped his hand and took a small step back, taking Melinda with me. "It's nice to meet you, and thank you for doing this, especially on such short notice."

"Anything for Melinda." His smile went wider.

"Um, yeah." I wasn't sure what to make of his comment.

"Can you give us a moment, Pastor?" Melinda politely asked.

"Sure. Whenever the two of you are ready. I'll be inside." With that, Pastor Johnson walked away.

"He's weird. And I don't like his aura," I said with certainty.

I went back to staring at the butterflies, but they were several rows back and a few plots to the left by now.

"He is weird but harmless," Melinda said as her attention was diverted toward the butterflies. "Why we're here, I just want to say hi to my family before we go in," Melinda expressed with watery eyes.

"Let's," I agreed.

Melinda linked our hands and led me to where the butterflies were hovering. The second we reached the three graves, the butterflies split into two separate masses. Like a dance, the smaller group flitted in a swirl-like pattern two rows away from where we stood.

"That's weird," Melinda said as she also watched the bugs.

"It sure is." And before I could say anymore, I saw the little boy. He stood stock-still at the end of the row while the butterflies were flying around him. "Do you see him?" I asked Melinda, pointing in his direction.

She glanced up from the headstones she was touching, with tears in her eyes, and stared across where the boy stood. "Are you talking about the butterflies?"

"No. The…" My words faltered when the boy placed his hands to his heart, a smile on his happy, infused face. He then walked in the opposite direction and disappeared into nowhere.

"What did you see?" she asked, looking around us.

I shook my head. "Nothing. Just a trick of the light."

Melinda accepted my answer with a nod. Even if she didn't, she hadn't let on.

I let Melinda have some time alone with her family. I walked over to where the boy once stood, and the butterflies danced about. There was a small open grave, which I assumed was where Cassie would be buried. To my utter surprise, next to Cassie's grave was my mother's plot, and next to hers was Marion's. I dropped to my knees, overwrought with emotions. I touched my mom's headstone, and warmth started to fill me. Through unshed tears, I read the headstone. *Here lies a beautiful soul. A loving mother and wife. Barbara Gene Whitlow Bishop. Born 1968 Died 2018.*

I ran my hand over the carved marble as tears let loose from my eyes. Melinda's warm hands on my shoulders pulled me back as she knelt down beside me. "This is your mamma," she said sweetly. There was no anger in her tone.

"Yes," I expelled out a hard breath.

She looked over at the open grave and smiled. "Then I'm glad your sister will rest in peace with her mother and Marion."

"I'm glad too." I stood, taking Melinda with me. I wiped away the tears that were a long time coming and said, "Let's go say goodbye."

Melinda leaned up and kissed me on my cheek. "Yes."

Hand in hand, we slowly walked back to the front of the church. I gave one final glance over to my mother's grave and saw the butterflies danced away.

THE END

A NOTE FROM THE AUTHOR

Dear Reader,

I want to thank you for buying Dance of the Mourning Cloak. This dark romantic thriller was originally part of an anthology called Dark Hollow Lake Collection One. But you have the extended edition of the story, which I hope you enjoy the connection Chase and Melinda has as they went through their journey.

I live for reviews. So please, help an author and leave one. Want to know more about me? Please sign up for my newsletter where you'll get sneak peeks of coming books, events and giveaways.

Smooches,

CJ

https://www.cjwarrant.com/newsletter

ABOUT THE AUTHOR

CJ Warrant is an award winning author of for dark romantic suspense and contemporary romance that pulls at your heart, makes you shiver with fear and has you falling in love. She's a lover of coffee, baking and family, but not always in that order. This is CJ Warrant's sixth book, with many more books to come.

Want more of CJ's world? Want to connect with CJ? Check her out on her social media. Come join her readers group, she'd love to hear from you.

www.cjwarrant.com

https://www.instagram.com/cjwarrant

https://www.twitter.com/cjwarrant

https://www.pinterest.com/cjwarrant

https://www.facebook.com/cjwarrantauthor

ALSO BY CJ WARRANT

Made in the USA
Columbia, SC
15 April 2021